CROSSROADS THROUGH TIME

CROSSROADS THROUGH TIME

A DIFFERENT CHOICE, AN ALTERED LIFE

Sheryl M. Frazer

ISBN-13: 9781973950103
ISBN-10: 1973950103
Library of Congress Control Number: 2017911828
CreateSpace Independent Publishing Platform,
North Charleston, South Carolina

DEDICATION

To my parents Sherald and Mary Ellen Sluka.
With all my love.

ACKNOWLEDGMENTS

I WANT TO thank those who spent the time to give me critical feedback on my first endeavor into this amazing, newfound love of the written word.

To my Dad, Sherald Sluka, for being one of my technical analysts, and was there from the start with help and guidance. Also, to my daughter Janet Alvarado. Honey, I'm so glad you received your degree in English!

Also, thanks to my sister and nurse, Sandy Goodwin, in helping me with all the medical lingo. Who knew the nurse changes a dressing and not a bandage? Sandy also gave me great feedback as I put each chapter together.

Then there were those who helped me by reviewing the completed story. It was important for me, because of the twists and turns that, what I intended for the reader to understand was indeed accomplished. Special thanks to my Mom, Mary Ellen Sluka, who was a wonderful reviewer and always gave me constant encouragement.

A big thanks to my dear friend Debi Miller, as well as my wonderful, supportive sisters, Susan Sluka-Kelly, Jo Ellen Huckabay, and Paige Scott Blackburn.

Finally, I would like to thank my husband Scott, and daughter Rachel who, from the start, gave me the time and space to see where writing could take me. Often picking up the slack as I lost time in the world of Genevieve.

I love you all!

TABLE OF CONTENTS

PROLOGUE

Tick tock, tick tock.

The familiar sound of time, as it consistently reminds us of
its relentless passing.
But time has no meaning in the eternal place, where a mere dream
opens a gateway of discovery, laying bare a reality never imagined.

PART ONE

THE PARTY

CHAPTER 1

─────── ❦ ───────

WHAT A BIRTHDAY
WHAT A FRIEND

GENEVIEVE WAS WELL aware her time was drawing near. She could feel the energy slowly being siphoned away. Soon the journey, one that we all are destined to take, would be hers. For some, the thought of venturing into the unknown is terrifying. What will be encountered? Will it be bliss or hell?

Genevieve had no trepidation of what was to come and even, one might say, had a feeling of excitement for the transition. It wasn't that she wouldn't miss all that she had. After all, here were her beloved friends, as well as this cherished oasis that had been her sanctuary for a very long time, but she felt at peace and trusted that moving on would be the next glorious adventure and everything would be as she had pictured it in her mind.

Looking at Genevieve, one might mistake her for someone who was catered to; with an aristocratic air, she was poised and elegant. However, she was the one, of all her friends, that was the most fearless and would take on any adventure because she only saw the fun in it, never the danger. She would often say, "Good grief! What good is life if you play it safe. That's not living at all!" Genevieve knew God had plenty of glorious angels. Many, she was sure, worked overtime on her behalf. But an angel she was not, more along the lines of one of God's little daredevils (minus the devil part, of course).

Genevieve had been married and, throughout a lifetime, experienced crazy highs and agonizing lows. In addition, the joy of motherhood was a roller coaster adventure in and of itself. But her children had all moved on, following their own paths now, and marriage was a precious memory.

Genevieve had an inviting, mature, allure about her. With upturned eyes of torrid green, framed by dark feathery lashes, she seemed to magnetize all who came near. Her olive skin, surprisingly, had minimal wrinkles except for the laugh lines around her mouth which only added to her beauty instead of stating a sign of age. Although petite, her posture resembled a prima ballerina, with long and wavy silver-gray hair that draped loosely around her shoulders.

With a transcendent love for God, Genevieve was unassuming, yet her boundless love was what drove her, propelling Genevieve forward to explore the wonders of life. Her unshakable faith armored her with knowledge that no matter what, everything would always be worth it--and it always was.

Today was Genevieve's birthday. As in copious times before, many had come to celebrate with their friend. It was an impeccable affair, as always, due to Rosa's incredible touch for detail.

Rosa and Genevieve were the closest of friends. Although Rosa was originally a caregiver for Genevieve, their relationship had grown over time. Now Genevieve not only depended on Rosa for her care, but trusted her remarkable ability to know what Genevieve needed way before Genevieve ever did.

Leaving the house to join the party, Genevieve was in awe, as the backyard had been transformed into a whimsical oasis at Rosa's hand. Closing the French doors behind her, she moved gingerly toward the sounds of murmuring voices and someone's outburst of laughter. *It must have been quite a joke!* Genevieve thought to herself.

Genevieve smiled in amusement as she looked up and observed the stars as they seemed to act like children, pushing and shoving each other in the attempt to impress her with their opulent brilliance. The tranquilizing music of Kishta could be heard softly in the background amid the peaceful aura of her Oriental garden. As Genevieve made her way over the small red bridge, she waved to the koy below that seemed indignant that she hadn't a nibble to feed them, their mouths groping at the air in insolence. Reaching the other side, the usually vibrant red Japanese maples on either side of the bridge seemed muted by the plethora of twinkling lights that decorated their delicate branches.

God, I love this place, she thought. The peace and euphoric atmosphere here always soothed her soul.

Round tables had been set with elegant dishware and several small framed pictures of Genevieve at different times throughout her life were on display at each. As the centerpiece, Rosa placed several tubular glass vases of various lengths together. Each had been filled with water and illuminated. Colorful rocks and shells glistened at the base while little Seahorses moved about or clung to the delicate green Anacharis plant ambling leisurely up the cylinder. "Seahorses," Genevieve whispered, "Simply magical!"

Then there was the birthday cake. Knowing Genevieve's love and fascination of galaxies and the omniscient splendor of the universe, Rosa had made a large, single layer round cake. She started by blanketing the entire cake in the darkest of chocolate icing. Then she frosted the center of the cake with a circle of snowy white and generously sprinkled it with edible white glitter. Emanating from the shimmering center several bright dotted lines of fiery blue, fuchsia pink, and honey yellow--all resembling small stars--curled around the center, moving outward to the edge of the cake. Rosa placed it strategically on a low rotating turntable so that, when peering down upon the cake, the most stunning spiral galaxy emerged before your eyes.

While the final few were arriving, Genevieve watched as Rosa stayed busy tending to the night's affairs and greeting guests as they arrived. Rosa's pure essence was of humility and graciousness. Her empathetic eyes were a calming light brown that beautifully complimented her flawless brown skin. Her long dark hair, was loosely braided, resting gently on one side. She was not much taller than Genevieve but had a bit more, as they say, to love. As a matter of fact, everything about Rosa was lovable. She was a natural at nurturing and protecting. Genevieve knew how very blessed she was to have Rosa by her side.

CHAPTER 2

STORIES TO TELL

LOOKING AROUND, GENEVIEVE counted twelve tables. All were occupied by her friends and family, some of whom she'd known forever. A handful of her more *endearing* guests were not the easiest ones to love, but those who often gave Genevieve the biggest difficulty. It was through them that she was forced to look at life, not only through her prism of reality, but theirs as well. Through them, she learned more keenly than anything else, that objectivity was one of the most essential elements in the understanding and compassion of others. Genevieve let out a little chuckle as she realized that Rosa, knowing full well, had placed several of them at her table.

Tonight, however, the table talk was full of laughter as one after another tried to "one-up" on their stories of past embarrassments while feasting on a heavenly five-course meal.

Kalinda, an old friend of Genevieve's, had just finished a hilarious story of an outhouse mishap when Genevieve turned around to see if everyone at surrounding tables were also having a good time. Every table was active with talk and laughter. Genevieve shook her head, amazed by all of those who had turned out in her honor.

As she continued to look around, Genevieve took notice of how many attending, had dressed for the occasion. There was no designated theme for the evening, yet many dressed as if they were at a worldly costume ball. Spying just a few, Tandi wore a colorful Moroccan kaftan and Aiko, looked elegant in a beautiful floral kimono. Henry chose to reflect his Spanish heritage with an elaborate Traje de Luce costume worn by the Torero (Matador), and Genevieve couldn't help but snicker watching Jay fiddle with his Scottish kilt. So many had chosen to reflect the vibrant diversity we all share but so

6

often is forgotten or ignored. It was such fun to see and added even more to the fanciful evening

After dinner was over, Genevieve stood and thanked everyone for coming, adding that their love and support, after such a long time, gave her pause. "Why you all put up with me and my shenanigans I'll never know, but thank God I've had you all by my side. You mean everything to me!" Then, without warning, Genevieve felt very faint. With a tinge of vertigo, she started to lose her balance and Rosa who was sitting at Genevieve's side, stood and held her waist to steady her. "Isn't Rosa incredible?" she hastily added to deflect any concern. "Please give her a round of applause for making this party so extraordinary!" Everyone came to their feet with a fervent roar of hands. When the cake was served, Genevieve was presented with the dazzling center of the cake, one candle lit. She giggled as everyone sang "Happy Birthday" then gathered just enough breath to blow out the flame.

After the last plate had been taken away and everyone was feeling quite content, Rosa leaned over to Genevieve and asked if she was feeling okay. Genevieve smiled and nodded her head, not wanting to spoil all that Rosa had planned, even though she was feeling unusually drained. Rosa got up and, after getting the attention of the group, asked if anyone had a good story to tell about Genevieve. More than a few hands went up. Genevieve could see then that the party was far from winding down.

Rosa's first pick was Jacob—Jay, for short. When Genevieve heard Jay's name she gave Rosa a quick glance and saw a grin on her face. They both knew they were in store for a rather embarrassing, but entertaining, monologue. Jay and Genevieve met when they both were in their early twenties. Genevieve had already taken beginner classes in cross-country skiing and wanted to learn more. On the first day of her class, she watched a tall, muscular guy next to her on the snow, fumbling with his poles when one smacked him in the face, knocking him backward into a snow bank. Being that he was standing in the back of the class only a few, like Genevieve, saw his blunder. Genevieve quickly turned away as Jay looked around to see if anyone noticed.

They soon became good friends for, although Jay had very little athletic ability, he had an infectiously optimistic nature. He also saw himself

7

as an alpha male and that got him into trouble--often. It didn't matter what endeavor Genevieve might try, whether it be rafting, horseback riding, or archery, if Jay found out about it, he would drop everything and join in. Genevieve admired his tenacity, but more often than she could remember, Jay ended up the wounded victim with Genevieve doctoring a cut on his head or wrapping a sprained ankle. Once she rushed to take him to the hospital emergency room for a nearly severed finger that got caught in the gear while rock climbing in Wye Valley. As Jay started to tell the story of the possessed arrow that got away from him, he looked over at Genevieve and gave a wink.

A little over an hour had passed. Two more brief but endearing stories were told before Amanda raised her hand and the fourth story began. Amanda, who had been a childhood friend, had the group rolling over in laughter as she described how Genevieve, at eight years old, had found an old, one-room shack not far from where she lived and decided to be the curator of the "Wonders of the Sea" museum. Living by the ocean in Squantum, Massachusetts, Genevieve had gathered starfish and small crustaceans--even a small lobster that had a mangled tail and had been tossed out by a local seaman. Proud as could be, Genevieve painted a seascape with a blue sky and billowy clouds inside the old shack. Hauling in some interesting rocks and even sand, she was determined to make her "museum" authentically real.

The one thing she didn't ever notice was the stench that permeated the little shack as her prized artifacts started rotting. When her father, a military man, came by one day to see what his daughter had been up to, he began to choke and gag as he peered in and saw Genevieve placing a new treasure strategically upon a sand mound. Although he praised her for her extraordinary imagination and hard work, he told her the odor was appalling and no one would want to enter such a smelly place. Well, that didn't stop Genevieve. The next week was Halloween so she changed her "Wonders of the Sea" museum into "The Wicked Sea Shack." She added a few ghosts and poured some ketchup around for effect. Then she told all the children she could find that for two cents they would "gag" at the smell and horrible sights within the wicked shack. Kids lined up for days just before Halloween to walk through the stinking hovel. Some, like Amanda, even paid twice to go through it again, embellishing on the experience when retelling what horrors were within. "Genevieve was always the one who found something fun to do, even on a rainy day." Amanda enthused.

Smiling, Genevieve tried to look engaged even though her mind kept drifting. Although she appreciated that her friends found her escapades intriguing and entertaining, she was becoming bemused, feeling the need to escape at least for a little while.

CHAPTER 3

COMFORT AND REFLECTION

INVENTING A REASON to leave, Genevieve touched Rosa's arm and whispered she needed to get something from inside the house and would be back shortly. Rosa petitioned to come along, but Genevieve told her she was quite fine on her own and she needed to do this alone. Rosa reluctantly watched as Genevieve slowly maneuvered her way around the tables, stopping for a few words with friends along the way.

As Genevieve moved down the stone path and started up the bridge towards the house, Kishta was still playing quietly. Like a soothing friend, the blissful symmetry of the music reverberated through Genevieve's core. She stopped for a few moments at the top of the bridge to relish the mastery of sounds. Rosa, watching all the while, sprung out of her seat, thinking it was a mistake to allow Genevieve to go on her own right now, but then, slowly sat back down after she saw Genevieve continue on her way.

Once inside all sounds were a distant muffle. Moving past a darkened living room, one could only make out some of the details. A beautiful large portrait of Genevieve hung over a pale blue love seat located near the entrance. The faint silhouette of a baby grand sat silently in the far-right corner while a large bookcase could be made out along the other. The fireplace along the left wall as well as the heavy leather chairs that sat in front of it were mostly obscured by the opaque darkness. Typically, a bright, inviting room, tonight the heavy drapes drawn over a large picture window next to the piano masked its elegant allure. With a cursory glance, Genevieve picked up the pace now, moving down a well-lit hallway until she arrived at a set of double doors. Opening and then closing them behind her, she leaned back and closed her eyes.

After a long pause, Genevieve opened her eyes and smiled. Before her, was *her* room, *her* oasis. A small sitting room filled like a giant scrapbook with mementos everywhere of special times, special trips. There was the modest pick-like tool from the Sudwala caves in South Africa and a perfectly preserved silkworm in a small gold case, to remind her of the time she learned to weave silk in India. Pictures covered the walls of memories long ago.

The room was lit only by the large fire in the fireplace to her left which Rosa tended to religiously. Above the fireplace was a rather large ornate clock, hands frozen in the twelve position. It was given to her by Rosa soon after they met. Broken from the start, Genevieve never heard the clock tick, even once. Now, looking up and surveying the clock's garish bejeweled frame, and overdone diamond studded face, Genevieve remembered with amusement opening up the anomaly and seeing Rosa beaming with excitement. Even the fact that it was broken didn't seem to faze Rosa a bit. She kept stressing that it was very rare, and she knew it was meant for Genevieve. Genevieve never understood why the clock wouldn't work though, as she was told all the parts seemed to be fine. Nevertheless, from that day on it adorned the small sitting room in silence. In time, Genevieve grew to cherish the old relic because Rosa did, and she cherished Rosa.

Genevieve glanced over at the overstuffed couch of eggshell white that sat in front of the fireplace, beckoning her to come and rest. But instead, she moved to the right. The entire room was wainscoted, with champagne colored upper walls and the lower paneling painted nautical blue. The walls displayed large and small pictures of moments that had great significance to Genevieve. A few of them had the typical smiling pictures of friends or family, but most were rather candid in nature as Genevieve cherished all of life as her tapestry, not just the posed moments.

Moving methodically along the wall, she raised her hand and gently touched a small black and white photo. In it she was standing, watching as a worker was fortifying a severely damaged portion of the Great Wall of China. Another magnified the lush green of a dense rainforest where she and a few others stood ankle deep in an ambling brook reaching for something beneath the water. Several native women, naked with painted tribal markings on their faces watched over them. Every picture an incredible story of its own.

As she slowly walked along the wall, she stopped and stared at a picture of herself standing on top of a cabin covered entirely by snow except for a tip of the chimney that was exposed at Genevieve's feet. She remembered that day so vividly. She was twenty years old and living in Sudbury, Ontario, Canada with her husband Edward and one-year-old daughter Gabriella. The couple had moved there from London, England six months prior when many living in their depressed area of the East End heard of the riches being mined in Sudbury and made their way westward in the hopes and promises of a prosperous life.

Despising the overcrowded suffocation they had left in England, they stayed far enough away from the burgeoning mining town of Sudbury, and instead chose a small cabin along the lower edge of the basin, unaware of the dangers that lurked in their precarious surroundings.

It was a frigid January afternoon and snow had been falling heavily for weeks. Edward, being one of the most dependable workers around was once again deep in the Murray Mine excavating nickel and copper ore. Little Gabriella was asleep after devouring a small bowl of barley soup, tiny pieces of bread, and her favorite apple pudding.

Genevieve had just sat down by the warmth of the fireplace when she felt the hair on the back of her neck stand up. A moment of unsettling *Deja vu* rolled through her body. She stood up. An almost undetectable sound that was strange, yet for some reason familiar, terrified her to her core. She didn't understand why but, just like an animal fleeing a forest fire, she instinctively grabbed her slumbering daughter, knowing she needed to get out of the cabin.

Trying to open the front door, she pushed with all her might, but the door seemed to be pushing back. Cumulative snow had again started to rise outside, even though Genevieve had cleared it a couple of hours prior. Now the snow was knee high outside the door. Little Gabriella began crying, sensing the fear her mother was emitting from every pore. Pushing against the door frantically with her back, Genevieve held the toddler tight in her arms. The door opened just enough for the two of them to squeeze out. The sound was quickly getting closer now, and Genevieve knew exactly what it was.

With precious little time left she struggled through the wet, debilitating snow to a closed-up shaft just a stone's throw away. This was one of the first mines excavated for its rich ore. Genevieve was told that when the initial blasting for the mine had been done, the cabin they now lived in had been built for supplies and a sort of way station for the workers. The mine's small entrance was very poorly covered, and without any struggle, she yanked the few boards from their decrepit posts. Grabbing Gabriella, she ran down a sloping tunnel. About 100 yards in, the shaft split. One side was open but dark, the other path must have collapsed, or was filled in on purpose, as it had large rocks piled most of the way up the opening.

Then she heard it. Choking with fear and unable to breathe, she heard the roar of the snow. It was deafening. She couldn't hear her daughter scream, even though Gabriella was pressed up against her, legs wrapped tightly around Genevieve's waist. As the ubiquitous tidal wave of snow smothered the world around her, she held close to her daughter, watching as the few, remaining rays of light coming from the opening were obliterated.

Just like that, it was over. Silence, except for the thunderous pounding sound of Genevieve's heart pulsing in her ears and little Gabriella, trying to catch her breath between inconsolable sobs.

But all she could think of was, *We're alive!*

Not knowing what might or might not be going on outside, Genevieve first stumbled her way toward the entrance on the slim hope that they could leave the way they came in. Although the snow had barely entered *into* the shaft, she knew by the density they were buried deep and attempting an escape that way was certain death. Feeling her way back to the split with Gabriella's precious little hands clinging tightly to her neck, Genevieve noticed a faint light coming from the tunnel that was full of rocks. With only pitch darkness coming from the open tunnel that led deeper into the mountain, she had no choice but to see if she could make her way up the jagged rocks to see where the light was coming from. With protest, Gabriella reluctantly released her constricting grasp so Genevieve could start to maneuver her way up the pile.

As she reached the top, she let out a muffled gasp as not to frighten Gabriella... again. On the other side, up a steep path was another entrance to the mine! Unobstructed, the entrance was spared the path of the avalanche, and so too were Genevieve and Gabriella's lives spared.

No one died that day, as the small avalanche covered not much more than their cabin and surrounding area, far from reaching the small mining town of Sudbury.

Turning, Genevieve moved to the back wall where a floor to ceiling window was covered by rich, satin-like drapery of midnight blue. She reached and pulled back one side of the drapes and stared out into the starry darkness.

Having a deep understanding of the symbiotic relationship humans have with God and the power that pure faith could unleash, she always seemed to understand that everyone was innately perfect--able to accomplish any feat, just like she did the day of the avalanche. She knew there was no such thing as original sin, but only the sinful error of allowing fear and doubt to overtake that perfection.

As Genevieve continued her gaze at the heavens, she remembered when she was asked to make a commencement speech at Westminster College, her alma mater, where, very late in life she received her degree in Philosophy.

As she stood in front of hundreds of students, many uncertain of the life ahead of them, she told them to not to be afraid of their future.

"We weren't born to travel the well-paved road. It is on the dirt path that we find new treasures. It's in those potholes that we find our strength and endurance and only then can we cherish our successes so much more. Remember that a firefly could never show off its brilliant light unless it were unafraid to fly through the darkness."

The next twenty minutes flew by as Genevieve spoke briefly of the "blessed potholes" in her life.

"One was public speaking itself," Genevieve exclaimed. "The first time I was ever asked to speak was at my daughter's first grade class about how to make a dough Christmas ornament. As I stood before fifteen wide-eyed darlings, I broke out into a full-on sweat. First graders! I thought. Getting all worked up to talk to little children. Right after that, I found ways to talk in front of people whether it was two, ten, or fifty, until my pothole filled in by facing the darkness of fear and doubt making me stronger."

In finishing, Genevieve spoke only of what she was certain, "Fear and doubt if left to fester, can turn masters into minions; goals and dreams into futility. God lives through *you,* and has no uncertainty of the master within, for God placed it there. Believe in yourself, and know this power! It will be your strength and the crushing blow to smother these insidious feelings and open a pathway to every success. I honor the master in all of you!"

The memory brought a smile to Genevieve's face. Not only did she receive a standing ovation that day, but it was a pinnacle moment of so many of her accomplishments.

Genevieve began to feel weaker and weaker. She grasped the drape hard for support as a slow emerging light from outside grew in intensity upon her. Facing into the salient brilliance, Genevieve seemed to be absorbing the light like a sponge. A penetrating love that goes beyond description, she felt porous as it filled every crevice of her being. Then, slowly, slumping to the floor, she released the drape, and the room returned to a dim glow.

Moments later Rosa entered, suspecting Genevieve would be found there she gasped, racing to Genevieve. When she lifted her, Genevieve let out a soft moan. Rosa moved her to the sofa, laying her gently down and covering her with the soft blue throw draped on the couch's end. Rosa knew now that her dearest friend would be leaving her very soon. With many talks together recently, Genevieve excitedly told Rosa of what she imagined she'd see and experience when her time there was over. It was remarkable as well as comforting for Rosa to see that Genevieve had only wonder for whatever lie ahead.

Genevieve opened her eyes to see Rosa smiling back at her. "Oh bother!" Genevieve whispered, "And I was so hoping to hear what story *you* had in mind to tell about little ole me."

Rosa let out a faint snicker. "Well, I suppose you've had enough embarrassment for today. But, boy the stories I could tell!"

Closing her eyes, Genevieve said, "Shush! We have to have something to tell at my next birthday!"

Rosa took a deep breath and let it out slowly.

Genevieve continued, "You know Rosa, you really outdid yourself. You have such a way of making my birthday's more and more enchanting! Speaking slower now with eyes still closed, "I hope you know how very deeply I love you."

Rosa brushed a strand of Genevieve's hair, from her face, not saying a word. Quiet filled the room as Genevieve lay silent. She could feel the touch of Rosa's warm fingers stroking her brow. It felt comforting, quiet, peaceful. There was a feeling of disembodiment, not moving in any particular direction, just floating, as if drifting into a dream. Slowly, snapshots began to appear--times in Genevieve's life. Was she seeing them with her eyes or was this vision in her mind? Where was she? She didn't know. The impressions before her were snippets of her life. Pivotal, life-changing moments. The ones that, by the choice made, can send your life soaring, or instead, can take you into a foreign nebulous type existence of despair.

Genevieve didn't panic or fight the phenomena as it progressed. Soon she found herself not observing but experiencing different times in her life, with all the knowledge and emotion as if it were happening at that moment. But, as each event unfolded the opportunity to experience the *other* choice was presented as well. A strange and extraordinary understanding was being gifted.

PART TWO

CHOICES AT 11 YEARS OLD

CHAPTER 4

AGE ELEVEN
CHOICE ONE

As the world around her came into focus, colors became vivid with an intensity and brilliance she had forgotten.

Genevieve knew herself to be eleven years old. Some might say too young to notice or appreciate the untouched natural splendor all around her, but nothing was further from the truth. As she sat on the front steps of her country home, looking out on a stunning spring morning, an explosion of wildflowers swept up and down the countryside around her. Genevieve let the smell of lilac and freesia overtake her senses. Beside her was the family cat, Tutu, the name Genevieve's mom had given her when she appeared out of nowhere at their front door one day as a kitten. An otherwise black cat except for the white zig-zag markings that ran around her lower body like a fluffy tutu, she often moved just like an elegant ballerina. Looking down, Genevieve couldn't help but smile, as Tutu seemed anything but graceful at the moment, lying asleep on her back with all legs spread outward, soaking up the morning sun.

All of a sudden the quiet was broken. Tutu was startled awake and sat with her ears perked. Genevieve heard voices just inside the screen door. She couldn't tell how many, but she could make out that they were talking about her father. Genevieve strained to hear what was being said. Although only hearing a hazy murmur, someone must have said something funny, as Genevieve heard laughter. However, a few moments later she could hear her mom crying.

At once, all the feelings flooded in, and Genevieve felt tears well up in her eyes. Her dad had just died.

Her father, Zeffran Clarke had been an infantryman in the Marines and had rarely spent time at home. Genevieve sensed the deep love she had for him, yet it was a love that was never to be satisfied. He would always say when he was home, that his family meant everything to him, but Genevieve, being eleven years old, couldn't understand, if that was true, why not quit his job and find another one so he could stay home like other fathers did.

Now, her life felt upside down. Just receiving word that her father had been killed in battle the day before, Genevieve was trying to grasp what "never see him again" and "gone forever" meant, as her mom kept repeating the phrases over and over in her despair.

As Genevieve closed her eyes, she could picture her father's handsome face smiling at her. His infectious laugh and upbeat attitude. Imagining she'd never see him again didn't seem real yet. Maybe it was because he wasn't there that much anyway, but right now, everything was feeling dismally abstract.

However, watching her mom fall apart was very real. Genevieve wanted desperately to make her mom happy and felt it was her responsibility to do so, but how?

Genevieve stood up, opened the screen door and came inside, Tutu scurrying in before the door closed. Her mom, Liv Clarke, looked up and wiped a tear away, then gave Genevieve a fleeting smile. Even with red and swollen eyes, Genevieve saw only love in her mom's beautiful hazel eyes and the warmth and tenderness of her smile. Liv was sitting on the couch in the living room with Genevieve's little sister, Teresa on her lap. Teresa, or Tess for short, had just turned three years old. How Genevieve wished she was her sister right now. Holding on to her worn-out bunny that only had one eye, Tess seemed to be oblivious to the pain and heartache surrounding her. On the other side of Genevieve's Mom was Sonia, her mom's good friend. Sonia's husband also was in the Marines. Genevieve was glad Sonia had come, as just her presence seemed like it was calming her mom somehow.

Also sitting in the room were Genevieve's neighbors, the Tuckers. Egan Tucker was Genevieve's age, and they were best friends. Often in trouble, the two seemed to be happiest daring each other to do stupid and occasionally dangerous tasks. Today, however, Egan sat quietly next to his dad. When he saw how upset Genevieve was, he got up and hugged her. Genevieve wasn't used to the sentimental side of Egan. In fact, she didn't know he even *had* that side. After a few awkward moments, they separated, and Egan took his place back, next to his dad.

Walking in from the kitchen were Aunt Melinda and Uncle Steven. Aunt Melinda was Liv's slightly older sister. While Genevieve's mom had a natural beauty, Aunt Melinda looked like she could be a model. She had long, dark hair, brown eyes and always wore beautiful clothes and bright lipstick. Uncle Steven was tall, big and very muscular. He always had funny jokes to tell, and Genevieve always looked forward to when he spent time with her and Tess. When Genevieve usually saw him, he was wearing a suit, but today he was just wearing jeans and a tee shirt. Uncle Steven and Aunt Melinda didn't have any children. Genevieve was told Aunt Melinda couldn't. But still, it was so much fun to visit them. They lived in a mansion that took hours and hours, just to travel there by car. There was a huge pool, and a gigantic stable with tons of horses. When the family would visit, Genevieve loved to spend as much time as she could, helping to feed and brush the horse's soft manes. The last time they were all together, Aunt Melinda let Genevieve ride the most beautiful one of all, named Haddie, for the first time!

Aunt Melinda spotted Genevieve and hurried over to give her a hug and a kiss. Genevieve could smell the spicy aroma of her perfume. "I wish I could take all your pain away," Aunt Melinda softly said, looking at her sister, Liv, then at Genevieve. The room became silent. Genevieve too, wished the pain would stop. Everything felt dark, like a nightmare from which she could not escape.

After an hour passed, the Tuckers said their good-byes. Egan seemed distant and off-balanced the entire time they visited, but then, that could be said about everyone. It was just that Genevieve wished she could have grabbed Egan and run somewhere, anywhere, so that they could just have fun again.

As the day went on and word got out, the base chaplain as well as other neighbors and friends, many with food, came by to express their condolences. By nightfall, only Aunt Melinda and Uncle Steven remained.

Tess had been fussy for the last few hours, and even Genevieve couldn't work her usual magic at making her sister laugh. For all their age difference, the two adored each other, Genevieve often taking care of Tess when her mom seemed distant and sad. Today was no different. Even though Genevieve's mom and Aunt Melinda were sitting in the kitchen, they both seemed oblivious to the needs of the girls, talking in a whisper so Genevieve couldn't hear what they were saying. Putting Tess in her highchair, Genevieve attempted to feed her little sister, but Tess, being overtired from the chaotic day, kept closing her eyes. Genevieve lifted her up and put her to bed without so much as a whimper.

Returning, Genevieve noticed for the first time that the kitchen was overflowing with all kinds of food. Typically, Genevieve would have devoured as many desserts as she could get away with, but tonight, everything looked and tasted like Brussel sprouts, Genevieve's least favorite food of all time. After picking at a plate of ham and potatoes, Genevieve stood and asked if she could go to bed. There was no argument. Genevieve went over to her mother and held her tightly in her arms. Both began to cry.

Genevieve felt desperation as her mom held tight and wouldn't let go. She kept her arms wrapped around her mom until the crying had subsided.

"You know how much I love you, right?" Genevieve's mom asked.

"I do, Mom. It'll be okay. I love you too." As Genevieve walked out of the room, she turned to see that her mom and Aunt Melinda had sat back down at the table and were holding hands. *It's good Aunt Melinda is here.* Genevieve thought.

While Genevieve lay in her bed, she could hear the muffled tones of her mom and Aunt Melinda's voices. It continued late into the night. Occasionally, she heard the deep bass sound of Uncle Steven saying a word or two. Eventually, Genevieve drifted off to sleep.

CHAPTER 5

FEELING RELIEF

THUMP, THUMP, THUMP.

"Tutu, stop," Genevieve mumbled. Tutu always slept above Genevieve's head at the top of her pillow. Her tail strategically placed to whack Genevieve in the forehead every morning. "No need for an alarm clock with you around, you silly cat" As she turned to look up at Tutu, Genevieve could swear the cat had a "who me?" snicker on her face.

Then it hit Genevieve as she remembered. She could feel her stomach tighten. It was still quiet in the house. Genevieve looked at the clock, and it was almost 9:00 a.m. *School.* Genevieve thought. *I should be at school.* But all she could do was lie there. She moved Tutu next to her and stroked the cat's head. Tutu closed her eyes and let out a comforting purr. Genevieve drifted back to sleep but woke a short time later when she heard people moving around.

All Genevieve wanted to do was stay in bed, but she wasn't sure if Tess was being attended to, so she threw the blanket back, causing Tutu to jump and screech in surprise. Smirking at her cat, she pondered, *I guess what goes around comes around.* Genevieve entered the living room, surprised to find Tess up, dressed, and munching on a piece of a banana. She was sitting in Aunt Melinda's lap. Even Tess' curly hair that always seemed hard to tame had been brushed and little clips placed nicely to keep the locks from falling in her face.

"Where is my mom?" Genevieve asked.

Aunt Melinda, wiping Tess' mouth responded, "She finally fell asleep a few hours ago. I heard Tess, so I got her up. She's all fed and ready for the day."

Genevieve had never seen a mothering side to her aunt. She too, was a lot of fun when they came for a visit, but she never struck Genevieve as maternal. "Thank you." Genevieve smiled.

Aunt Melinda put Tess down, and they both watched as Tess walked over to Genevieve and reached for Genevieve to pick her up. As Genevieve bounced Tess around on her lap, as she often did, making Tess laugh hysterically, she couldn't help noticing Aunt Melinda's wistful stare.

Tess' infectious laughter got Uncle Steven up. "Those giggles are the best medicine in the world!" He said. Bending down, he gave Genevieve a kiss on the cheek, then picked up Tess, and instead of giving her a kiss as well, he put his lips to her cheek and blew hard making a funny sound that got Tess laughing all over again. Within a minute, all four of them were on the floor, rolling around, trying to tickle each other.

Genevieve brushed a quick tear away. It felt good to laugh. Until now, she hadn't fully realized that even before her dad had died, there always seemed to be a cloud of sadness around their house. Genevieve did everything she could think of to make her mom happy, but it was only when her dad was around, that her mom was full of life.

When Genevieve felt the sadness of her mother too overwhelming, she looked for an escape. One such escape was spending time on the hillside by herself, or sometimes with Tess, watching in quiet anonymity as nature was a flutter all around. The other was playing with her gutsy friend Egan. She also enjoyed time spent at his home, with his family. It was so...normal. His mom loved to cook, and always seemed to be busy in the kitchen. On weekends, when Genevieve was able to visit, Egan's mom would try to rouse a good conversation with both of them, but Egan only spent as much time "chatting" as it took to scarf down whatever snack his mom was offering, then pulling Genevieve away to their latest escapade. Egan's dad worked at the courthouse, and occasionally Genevieve saw him wearing a suit and tie, looking very important. But most the time, on the weekends, he dressed in casual jeans and tee shirt, sitting and talking to his wife as she maneuvered around the kitchen or if Egan could be corralled long enough, he'd join in a game of darts or horseshoes in the backyard.

Now, with Aunt Melinda and Uncle Steven, it felt like one of those escapes.

After everyone had eaten breakfast, they moved outside, sitting around in chairs on the large front porch. Aunt Melinda asked Genevieve what was going on at school and Uncle Steven couldn't pass up the chance to tease her about the hug from Egan. Aunt Melinda told Genevieve about the new horse they bought and a puppy they were going to get as soon as it was old enough to leave its mother. "It's the cutest little golden retriever!" Aunt Melinda said. "A purebred of course." Genevieve had no idea what that meant but wished she could have a puppy.

CHAPTER 6

FINDING STRENGTH

HEARING THE SCREEN door, Genevieve looked up to see that her mom was awake and coming to join everyone outside. She first walked over and gave Genevieve a kiss then picking up Tess, walked over to a rocker near them and sat down, giving Tess a kiss on her head. "Are you okay, Mom?" Genevieve asked, to break the awkward silence. Watching, she saw her mom and Aunt Melinda look at each other. Genevieve sensed that something was up.

Looking back at her daughter, Liv began, "Genevieve, you are my angel, you know that? Not only have you watched over your sister, but you've watched over me more times than I can count, and it's been so terribly unfair to you. You're only eleven years old for God's sake!" Tears began to fill Liv's eyes.

Genevieve looked around at her aunt and uncle, unsure of where all of this was going, but both just looked lovingly at her.

Liv continued, "Genevieve, I'm not well. I've been sad for a long time, and now I can't help but feel that my life is over with your father gone. I know I shouldn't feel that way. I have you, my beautiful girls, and no one could love you more, yet I'm not able to even care for myself right now, much less both of you, and you deserve so much more. You can't...I won't let you live like this anymore. I think it's best, that after the funeral, I go to a hospital where there are doctors who can help me."

Genevieve couldn't believe what she was hearing. "You can't leave us!" Genevieve said automatically. "I don't mind taking care of you and Tess! I'm old enough, really! Besides, where would we go?" Genevieve could feel the tears moving down her face and angrily brushed them away.

In a calm and composed voice, Liv said, "I have been talking to Aunt Melinda and Uncle Steven, and they would love to have you stay with them. At least until I feel better."

Reeling in chaotic thought, as one question after another entered her mind, the only thing Genevieve could utter was, "How long will that be?"

Her mom slowly moved her head from side to side, "I don't know, Love."

Genevieve's lip quivered, but she held back her tears. Tess looked at her big her sister in bewilderment as if she was about to cry. "It's okay Tess," Genevieve said. "It's okay" Then Genevieve ran inside, fell on her bed and cried uncontrollably.

Giving her niece some time to process the latest bombshell, but not too much time to agonize in guilt and feel abandoned, Aunt Melinda made a sandwich for Genevieve and brought it to her room. "May I come in?" Genevieve was sitting at the head of her bed, holding Tutu and stroking her fur. Tears were gone, but her red eyes remained. She looked up at Aunt Melinda and gave a nod. Aunt Melinda put the sandwich on the nightstand and said, "I thought maybe a little to eat might make you feel better." The only taker was Tutu, making her way quickly to the sweet aroma of food. Genevieve just watched as Tutu examined the unexpected treat before taking a big bit of roast turkey.

"I just want her to be happy," Genevieve said. "I guess if that means leaving us, then I'll do it. I love you and Uncle Steven, but I can't help thinking that Mom will be so lonely without us. She depends on me." Genevieve just kept staring, blankly at the cat, "Will she be okay Aunt Melinda?"

Putting her arm around Genevieve's shoulders, Aunt Melinda kissed her head. "I love your mother very much, and I've always protected her, maybe too much."

Genevieve looked at her aunt, "I don't know what you mean."

Now, Aunt Melinda had that far-away look, "Even as a child, your mom never thought she was capable of doing anything on her own. She never tried, expecting me to handle everything for her. Our mother, your grandmother, would never coddle her in that way, but I did. So, she always depended on me or anyone she could find to handle things for her. I was so surprised when Liv ended up marrying your father because I knew she'd be on her own most of the time, but then I thought, she must feel able, or she wouldn't commit to being a career soldier's wife. Can you understand what I'm saying so far, Genevieve?"

As Genevieve nodded her head, puzzle pieces were coming together. Genevieve wondered too, *Why would Mom choose someone who wouldn't be around to take care of her. Did Dad know how badly she needed him?*

Aunt Melinda continued. "The thing was, they fell in love and married so fast, your mother didn't know what life would be like until two months after they were married and he headed overseas. From then on, a little piece of her broke each time he was sent away again. I asked her many times to come and live close to me, but, for whatever reason, she wanted to stay here. So, over the years I've done what I could, but she needs more help than I, or you can give her."

Genevieve wanted to have someone to blame for all of it, but, now it seemed both her parents saw something in each other that wasn't really there--stability. "Can I bring Tutu with us? Genevieve asked as she glanced over and saw the cat licking her paw and then brushing it over her face.

"You've got it!" Aunt Melinda said. "Hope she'll get along with the new puppy. You'll have to help me name him. He should be ready to take home by the time we get back. I'll see how your mom is doing. Come out and talk to her. You two need to be together right now."

As Aunt Melinda left the room, Genevieve felt hurt and optimistic all at the same time. *It will be so hard to leave here. I'll miss my friends and Egan so much! But, maybe Mom will get better, and then we can come back. At least we can stay with Aunt Melinda and Uncle Steven. I hope it will all be okay.*

After a few minutes, Genevieve went back outdoors. Everyone was still sitting on the front porch. Tutu followed Genevieve and, spotting a Blue Jay in the yard, sprinted, like the big hunter she thought she was, but Genevieve had yet to see a single bird victimized by the ferocious feline. Puzzled that the bird had escaped her capture, Tutu sat bewildered for a few moments, then turned and moseyed over to her usual sunny spot on the porch and laid down.

Tess was having a good time with Uncle Steven, allowing him to build a block tower, then swiping her hand and knocking them all down. Uncle Steven looked totally surprised every time, making Tess laugh.

Aunt Melinda was sitting next to Liv. As Genevieve looked at her mom, she felt good that her mom would get the help she needed. She walked over and sat on her mother's lap, wrapping her arms around her neck. Genevieve sensed relief and saw a peacefulness with her mother now. Liv kissed Genevieve and rocked her for a long time as Genevieve savored the little time left in her mother's embrace.

CHAPTER 7

SAME EVENT
A DIFFERENT CHOICE

HOW BEAUTIFUL, GENEVIEVE thought.

Looking out on the stunning spring morning, eleven-year-old Genevieve sat on her front porch, admiring the explosion of wildflowers that swept up and down the countryside around her. Breathing in the refreshing aroma of flowers surrounding her, and smiling at her sprawling cat, Tutu, that lay beside her, Genevieve sensed a familiarity.

Within moments, the heartache of her father's passing took the path of sadness as well the sense of his abandonment, yet, Genevieve's own feelings of responsibility haunted her. As she entered the house and joined family and friends, everything felt foreign and unfamiliar. Everyone, with their sorrowful faces, made Genevieve want to grab her friend Egan, who was there with his family and escape the gloom that had invaded her home. But, she would never do that to her mother.

When Aunt Melinda remorsefully remarked, "I wish I could take all your pain away." Genevieve wanted the same, but knew it was her job; it had always been her job, trying to make her mom happy again.

Throughout the day, Genevieve checked on her mom, almost hourly, interrupting conversations she was having with her friend Sonia as well as Aunt Melinda. It was Genevieve who cared the most for her mother, and she wouldn't shirk her responsibility now.

That evening, after she had put her little sister to bed, Genevieve wanted to go to sleep as well. Utterly drained, she wanted nothing more at that moment than to crawl into bed and sleep forever. But instead, Genevieve went back to the kitchen, one last time for the day, to check on her mom. As she entered, she saw Aunt Melinda and her mom talking quietly. A feeling of love and compassion for her aunt swept over her. *I wish Aunt Melinda lived near us.* Genevieve thought. Looking over the plethora of food choices, none that had the slightest appeal, Genevieve placed a piece of ham and some cold mashed potatoes in front of her and stared at them for a few moments. Picking up her fork, she poked the piece of meat, but then placed the fork back down and murmured, "If it's okay, I think I'll go to bed now." As she looked over, her mom gave her a warm smile and motioned for Genevieve to come over. Genevieve got up and held tight to her mother.

"You know how much I love you, right?" Genevieve's mom asked.

"I do Mom," Genevieve stated. "It'll be okay. I'll always be here for you."

Aunt Melinda sat quietly nearby. As Genevieve held her mother, Aunt Melinda looked at Genevieve and silently mouthed, "I love you too."

After leaving the kitchen and heading to her bedroom, Genevieve noticed Uncle Steven sitting alone in the living room. He motioned for her to come over.

"Hey Genevieve, do you know why your cat TuTu doesn't dance?" Genevieve shrugged. Uncle Steven held up two fingers, "Because, she has **two too** many feet! Or, here's a better one: Because she only knows how to cat-walk!" Genevieve gave a little smile and sat next to him on the couch. Uncle Steven felt encouraged and continued. "Why do cats get to stay inside the house more often than dogs?"

Genevieve decided to engage her uncle. After a few moments to think, she said, "Because dogs are too ruff?"

Uncle Steven looked surprised, "Cool answer! I was going to say because cats are better at purr-suasion."

Genevieve couldn't help but chuckle. "I like that better." Whenever Genevieve visited her uncle, the two would try to outdo the other with made-up jokes. She appreciated his valiant effort, but Genevieve's head hurt, and exhaustion had overtaken her. Giving her uncle a kiss on the cheek, Genevieve stood back up. "I love you Uncle Steven."

Replying quickly, Uncle Steven shot back, "Right back at you, Sweetness. See you in the morning."

CHAPTER 8

UNSTABLE FOOTING

GENEVIEVE HAD A fitful night's sleep, and now Tutu was walloping her on the forehead with her tail, waking her to the day, as well as reality.

Figuring her mom must be letting her stay home from school since it had never been discussed, she escaped back to slumber for a while longer, until she heard voices outside the room. Tearing herself away from the warmth and comfort of her bed, Genevieve slipped on a robe and headed for the source of the sound and to check on Tess.

Genevieve stood in the living room doorway for a long moment, watching her Aunt Melinda and sister interact. They looked comfortable together. Little Tess looked like she was dressed for church, wearing her blue frilly dress and adorable clips in her hair. At first, it made Genevieve smile, but then it felt wrong somehow, that Tess could be so happy with anyone other than Mom or herself. Although Genevieve loved to be around her aunt, she had never experienced a maternal side to her, and it felt rather conflicting.

"Where is my Mom?" Genevieve asked in a casual tone. Aunt Melinda looked up with a broad smile. Genevieve had never noticed how much her aunt and mom resembled each other until now. She swallowed hard, choking back all the emotions that started to bubble up within her.

"She finally fell asleep a few hours ago," Aunt Melinda replied.

When Genevieve sat down on an overstuffed easy chair, Tess came over and sat with Genevieve. Giving Tess a kiss, she started bouncing her on her lap, making Tess scream and giggle. Looking over at her aunt, Genevieve couldn't help but wonder what her aunt was thinking. She seemed to be looking at the two of them, and yet she seemed far away. "Are you okay. Aunt Melinda?"

Blinking back into focus, Aunt Melinda mused, "I was just thinking how special it is to have a sister that you're close to."

Before long, Uncle Steven was up and making everyone laugh. Genevieve's feelings of responsibility subsided as she lost herself in unrestrained laughter, something she hadn't done in a very long time.

When breakfast was finished, all four had moved to the outside porch to enjoy the beautiful day and keep the noise down so Liv could sleep. Uncle Steven and Aunt Melinda did their best to distract Genevieve, talking about a new puppy they were getting, as well as asking her about school and friends. It got Genevieve wondering if Egan would be coming over to see her after school. She closed her eyes, picturing the two of them playing their usual tricks on each other. Then, she heard the screen door and opened her eyes. Her mom was up and coming to join them.

The smile Genevieve still held, slowly diminished as she watched her mom. Genevieve had hoped her mom would be a bit happier today, but she could tell that something was off. It was a look Genevieve couldn't read. "Are you okay, Mom?" Genevieve asked.

Her mom looked exhausted. Giving Genevieve a kiss, she picked up Tess and sat down. Everyone's attention was on Liv. As her mom spoke, a panic slowly enveloped all of Genevieve. Words of "not being well" and leaving them to "go to a hospital" were more than Genevieve could accept. "You're only sad now." Genevieve blurted. "It will get better, you just need some more time!"

Her mom started to interject, "But Genevieve, Honey..."

There was no "but" anything in Genevieve's mind. "I don't mind helping, you have to believe that!"

Liv watched her daughter in bewilderment. "I just want you to be happy Genevieve. If I get some help, I can be the mom you and Tess deserve."

Genevieve heard nothing through the intense feelings of abandonment. "I won't let you go, Mom! You can't do this to me. You're all I have!" After a long pause, Genevieve came close to her mother and said, "If you *really* love us, you won't leave!" Tess started crying. Genevieve swung the screen door open and ran to her room sobbing.

Genevieve could hear her sister crying outside, but she didn't care. Nothing mattered. Everything Genevieve did to make her mom and Tess happy didn't seem to matter. As she held Tutu, crying, her tears wet the feline's fur. Still, Tutu sat quietly, looking up at Genevieve as if she understood and sensed Genevieve's need to be with her.

A few minutes later Aunt Melinda came in with a sandwich. "I thought maybe a little something to eat might make you feel better."

Genevieve glanced over at her aunt, "Only my mom can do that."

Aunt Melinda sat on the bed with a pensive look. "You're a lot like me, you know that Genevieve?"

Still staring at Tutu, "I don't see how," Genevieve murmured.

"Well, I care about your mom, just like you do. I have all my life. I've always wanted her to be happy in the same way you do. But sometimes caring means letting go."

Before Aunt Melinda could continue, Genevieve looked up and gave her an angry stare. "We're nothing alike then! Genevieve shouted. Tutu, jumped from the bed, startled. "If I let go I'll have nothing! Please leave!"

Liv had been standing just outside the doorway. When she entered, Aunt Melinda stood, giving her sister a soulful look. They held hands momentarily, then Aunt Melinda walked out. Genevieve sat on the bed, her lip was quivering. She looked at her mom, trying not to cry, she was *so* tired of crying. Liv sat next to her, and wrapped her arm around Genevieve's waist.

"Okay," Liv said matter-of-factly.

"Okay? What do you mean?" Genevieve countered.

"I'll stay. I hate to see you like this. Maybe I do just need more time." Genevieve turned and gave her mom the tightest hug she could muster. Liv stroked Genevieve's hair. "I love you, Genevieve. Don't ever forget that."

When they both came back outside, Liv announced she would be staying at home after all.

Aunt Melinda protested, "Liv, no! The girls will be just fine with us. Take some time to feel better, please!" Genevieve gave her mom a worried look.

Liv looked down at Genevieve, "It's okay Melinda. I'll be fine."

Aunt Melinda tried the rest of the day to persuade her sister that she needed help for her depression, but Genevieve stayed close to her mom, in case she might change her mind, and was relieved when her mom held firm.

The next day, Genevieve's dad was going to be arriving at the mortuary. The funeral was planned for the following day. *One last day to be sad.* Genevieve thought.

CHAPTER 9

I WILL LOVE YOU FOREVER

As GENEVIEVE WATCHED her father's casket being lowered into the ground, a flood of emotions overtook her. She remembered the last time she saw him alive. He was so happy to be home, but couldn't stop talking about the thrill of combat, how it gave him such satisfaction when his mission was accomplished.

Genevieve remembered watching, as her mom shook her head, saying, "There has to be something wrong with you if killing people gives you such happiness." Then looking defeated, her mom went to the bedroom and slammed the door with her dad in hot pursuit. It took a couple hours, but by the time they came back out, her mom and dad were laughing and giggling as if they didn't have a care in the world.

As Genevieve's lip began to tremble she thought, *You sure had a way - a special way about you, Dad.* Genevieve had not truly grasped the finality that was now before her eyes. "I love you, Daddy," she said softly. As tears fell once more, Liv, hearing her daughter, reached over and kissed her head.

That evening Aunt Melinda and Uncle Steven were getting ready to leave. Aunt Melinda wanted to stay, but Liv insisted she was fine and that she was sure there must be more pressing things for them to attend to back home.

Before leaving, Aunt Melinda took Genevieve aside and gave her a warm embrace. "I truly understand your love for your mom. She's very blessed to have you, Genevieve. I want you to please understand it was never my intention to take her away from you, although it may have seemed that way. I love her, and I love you. If you ever need me, I'll come right back, okay?"

Genevieve had felt somewhat betrayed by her aunt, but now, as her aunt held her tight, Genevieve felt her genuine love and concern for her. She wanted to say she was sorry for the way she acted, but the words remained stuck in

Genevieve's throat. "Okay, Aunt Melinda. I hope we can come and see you soon. I can't wait to see your new puppy."

Aunt Melinda smiled, "Ah, yes, our little puppy. I got word yesterday that he's ready to be picked up. It would have been great to have you help with the little guy. I hope I'm up for the task!"

Again, a little regret tugged at Genevieve. "As soon as Mom is feeling better we'll come help."

When it was finally just the three of them left in the house, it felt odd, lonely even, although it was no different than before. Genevieve sat alone in the living room. *Mom is spending a really long time putting Tess down for the night.* Finally, Liv entered and sat next to Genevieve. Genevieve could tell her mom had been crying. Her eyes were red, but Genevieve pretended not to notice.

Kissing Genevieve on the cheek, "It's been a long day," Liv said.

"I know. I'm pretty tired myself," Genevieve agreed.

Liv wrapped her arms around Genevieve. After a long silence, Liv whispered, "I miss your dad so much. I don't know why this has happened." Genevieve had no answer for her mom but felt deep anguish as they held each other tight. Liv continued, "If you're okay, I think I'll go to bed now." Genevieve nodded. Liv walked to her room and closed the door.

As Genevieve was heading to her room, she peered in to check on Tess. While she watched her sister sleep, Genevieve tried to convince herself, *We'll all be happy again soon.* Closing the door quietly, Genevieve walked over to her bedroom and fell onto her bed, the last thing she remembered was Tutu jumping up and taking her usual spot at the head of the bed.

As day broke, Genevieve could feel the warmth of the sun shining on her face as she lay with her eyes still closed. *Why is the sun, and not Tutu waking me up?* Genevieve thought. She reached above her, but Tutu wasn't there. Prying her eyes awake, Genevieve looked at the clock. Barely 6:00. *Where is that cat?* She wondered. Getting up, she heard Tutu meowing. Following the sound, she found the cat outside her mom's bedroom. "Shhhh, you silly cat. You'll wake Mom." Genevieve started to walk away, expecting the cat to follow, but instead, Tutu let out another loud meow, this time getting Genevieve's attention. As she looked back, the cat was crouched down, nose up against the space at the bottom of the door. Genevieve slowly moved back over to her mom's bedroom. Tutu looked up at Genevieve and let out another strange meow. Genevieve stared at the door, her heart now throbbing.

Knock. "Mom, can I come in?" Silence. Genevieve opened the door. The room was dark, quiet. "Mom?" Genevieve wanted to leave, but it was like something was compelling her to step closer and closer to the bed. As she moved to the side of the bed, she felt something below her foot. Looking down, Genevieve's blood ran cold. An empty pill bottle. When she grabbed her mom's arm, it felt icy, rigid. Genevieve shook her head in disbelief, backing up then stopping at the door, before letting out a crushing, tormented howl. Running back to her mom, Genevieve laid next to her, hoping she was wrong; that her mom was just sleeping. But as she looked at her mom's face she knew. There was a peacefulness about Liv now. When Genevieve touched her mom's face she had a strange, yet comforting feeling she didn't understand. Was her mom trying to let her know something? Genevieve could hear Tess crying in the other room but held her mom as if nothing else in the entire world mattered as she thought, *I hope you can finally be happy Mom. I'm sorry I wasn't enough, I'm sorry for everything.* Then Genevieve whispered in her mom's ear, hoping she could hear, "I'll love you forever."

PART THREE

CHOICES AT 17 YEARS OLD

BACK AT THE PARTY...

KEEPING WATCH OVER Genevieve as she lay in an apparent sleep, Rosa heard a knock at the door, and upon answering it, Biju, one of the many friends attending the party and long retired physician was standing there. Rosa didn't need to say anything, Biju knew. As he walked over to where Genevieve lay, he could see the paleness upon her face and slow, shallow breathing.

Since she seemed comfortable for the time being, he asked if he could stay and keep Rosa company. Rosa gave him a warm hug and let him know she would be happy if he did.

Meanwhile, Genevieve had no time to reflect on what she was experiencing, nor did she realize the significance of what the alternative choice would mean for her in the end. But, caught in a dream from which she couldn't awaken, she opened her eyes, and she was seventeen.

CHAPTER 10

————— ❦ —————

AGE 17
CHOICE ONE

THE BAGS WERE packed and placed near the large entrance. Three large trunks and seven big suitcases! *What does Aunt Melinda think, that we're going to move to England!* Genevieve thought as she sat on the last step of the open stairway.

Everyone looked forward to summer, as Aunt Melinda and Uncle Steven used that time to show Genevieve and Tess how incredible their world was, as well as escape the heat of Arizona. Every trip was well thought out with every detail managed to perfection by Aunt Melinda. From their very first trip as a family, when they went to Japan, Tess saw everything as "Exotic." The people were exotic, the buildings were exotic, even bicycles were exotic, and although Tess overused it at times, Genevieve actually loved the term.

Now everyone was going to England, northeastern England to be precise. Aunt Melinda had given Genevieve a Geordie Dictionary, saying, "Although we'll technically be in England, I've been told the people in the area have more of a Scottish dialect. You might want to study up a little on a different way of speaking English. At the very least, keep it handy."

Since Uncle Steven had business there, the family decided it would be a perfect time to spend a couple of summer months in another *exotic* land. Uncle Steven was in real estate. Aunt Melinda said he was very successful because he had an uncanny sense of knowing a good deal from a bad one. So, he and a few other investors were heading to the Northumberland coast and Bamburgh, England. All Genevieve knew was that it was supposed to be a beautiful coastal area and it had a castle. *Now that's exotic!* Genevieve thought to herself.

Hearing some commotion outside, Genevieve walked out front. Tess, and Egan, their golden retriever sat on the grass in front yard, watching as a large truck stopped in the circular driveway near the house. The driver loaded up Uncle Steven's golf clubs as well as the three trunks and several suitcases which were too big to fit in the limousine, then drove off to the airport.

The limo would be full today as Egan would be taking the trip as well. When Genevieve and Tess first came to stay with their aunt and uncle, it was Genevieve who got to name their new puppy, and the only boy name she wanted to call him, was Egan, the friend she left behind. So, Egan, it was. It was always so hard to leave their dog when they would go on their summer vacations; he was so much a part of the family. This time, because of the length of the trip, Aunt Melinda made special preparations so Egan could also come along.

Just as the transport truck faded from sight, the limo came around, and Geoffrey waved at the girls. Geoffrey was Uncle Steven's chauffeur but much more than that. Uncle Steven and Aunt Melinda invited Geoffrey to all the family outings, and Uncle Steven seemed to ask for his advice a lot. An older gentleman, Geoffrey was quiet and unassuming. He never mentioned any family of his own. Genevieve always thought of him as a grandfather figure, never knowing either of hers. Learning that Geoffrey would be traveling with them this time, the family felt complete.

The trip to England seemed shorter than Genevieve thought it would be, probably because of how excruciatingly long it took when they went to Africa the previous year. Still, Genevieve knew how privileged she was, to be able to see places she never even knew existed.

By the time they arrived at the Wainsworth Estate, just south of Bamburgh, it was almost dusk. The air was damp and refreshing, quite a welcoming contrast from the hot dry heat Genevieve had just left in Arizona. As everyone piled out of the car, Egan bolted, running back and forth with an explosion of energy. Being caged was not something he had ever experienced before. Genevieve and Tess both tried to grab his leash as he whirled by them, but he was having too much fun with his new-found freedom to be constrained. While Geoffrey talked to a porter, who was unloading the luggage everyone else started for the entrance. After seeing that no one was chasing after him anymore, Egan reluctantly followed, his leash dragging behind him.

On the drive over from London, Aunt Melinda talked about the property where they would be staying. Once the home of a baron in the mid-1800's, it had gone into disrepair and had been abandoned. Some local businessmen bought it from the bank and transformed it into a beautiful upscale hotel. The main building was dripping with rich history. Lavender wisteria, in full bloom, covered the towering walls. The pleasant sweet smell drew Egan closer, sniffing at the delicate flowers, but Uncle Steven startled everyone, yelling for Egan to return. Not knowing the particular variety of plant, the flowers could be edible or poison. Uncle Steven assumed it was safe, but didn't want to take any chances.

The main lobby was open, bright and inviting. You could smell heavenly aromas of fresh bread and a hint of garlic from the nearby dining room. There was a beautiful open staircase, leading to guest rooms upstairs. However, Uncle Steven had chosen a three-bedroom cottage near the lavender court-yard just south of the main building. It would accommodate all five of them as well as provide more space for Uncle Steven to do his work.

Once the check-in was finished, a young man, looking a little older than Genevieve came over and said he'd lead everyone to the cottage and assist with the luggage. Genevieve noticed how polite he was when he addressed her as 'Miss.' It was a term she rarely heard where she came from, yet it sounded so refined and respectful coming from him. He seemed a bit shy, but as she followed behind him, she noticed how he kept looking back at her, just as she too, kept her eye on him. He was close to a foot taller than Genevieve, with crystal blue eyes, and short dark hair. Genevieve adored his Scottish accent and understood everything he said. *Maybe I won't need that dictionary after all,* she thought.

As they walked toward the cottage, Genevieve could not be silent any longer. "What's your name?"

The young man turned and stopped, making everyone come to a stand-still behind him. "Everyone calls me Teddy, Miss." He gave a slight bow of his head, then turned and continued down the pathway.

But, a few steps later, "Do you work here all the time?" Genevieve inquired.

Again, Teddy turned and stopped. Tess, not paying attention this time, ran right into the back of her sister, propelling Genevieve forward who almost stumbled into Teddy. As Genevieve gained her balance, she sheepishly raised her head to see that Teddy was now just inches away. Brushing her long hair back, she stood straight, and gave Teddy a surprised, wide-eyed look.

Staring back at her, he began to answer her last question. "Not all the time, Miss. I just help oot when I'm needed. My fatha was the gentleman who assisted your family upon check-in. My family lives on the property. Jake, the porter, has been a bit under the weather for the past few days, so I've been filling in for him." Before Teddy turned back around this time, he paused, continuing his stare at Genevieve. When she had nothing to say, he gave her a half-turned smile, exposing a deep dimple in his cheek. She could feel a sudden flush in her face as she gave him a quick smile in return.

When they arrived, the cottage was already lit. Teddy moved the luggage to the appropriate rooms and checked to make sure there were plenty of linens. Before leaving, he pointed to a table where a plate of sweets and a large porcelain teapot with cups sat, "Welcome to Wainsworth Estate. Please enjoy the biscuits and hot tea."

As Genevieve looked over, she smirked, "You mean cookies?"

Teddy, put up his forefinger, remembering what Americans call them, "Aye, yes Miss, I'm sorry, cookies. The dining room will be open for another two hours if you're feeling hungry. Please ring the front desk for any needs ye may have. I'm here at your disposal." Genevieve tried to act casual as Teddy gave her one last look before he left.

Once he closed the door, she briskly walked to the window and looked out, just as he looked back and gave a quick wave.

Aunt Melinda smiled, "He's a handsome fella, don't you think Genevieve? Tess chimed in, "You were drooling all over yourself. It was gross!"

Genevieve looked insulted but still watched him as he walked back to the main lobby. "I was not drooling! I was just being nice, and I wanted to listen to him talk. I love that accent!"

Uncle Steven rolled his eyes. Then, speaking with a poor imitation, "Well, Miss, I'm quite famished, and these biscuits just won't fill me up. Let's all get freshened up a bit in the loo, and make our way over to have that delicious smelling fillet of beef, some potato cakes and rhubarb custard for dessert!" Tess and Aunt Melinda clapped simultaneously.

Geoffrey, not having a chance to visit the restroom earlier, remarked with urgency, "I don't mind being the first one to try out the loo!" Then he hurried over and shut the door. Genevieve strolled slowly over and tried out one of Teddy's biscuits, feeding one to Egan as well.

CHAPTER 11

─── ⁓⌒⁓ ───

TEDDY CRUSH

THE NEXT MORNING, Uncle Steven and Geoffrey were up before dawn to meet with a few people in Bamburgh. Geoffrey had already taken Egan out to do his business and to get some exercise, so the cottage was peaceful until Egan started barking and scratching to get out the door. Genevieve reluctantly slipped out of bed to see why the dog was so excited. Outside, on the window ledge a small, rusty colored squirrel sat, staring up at her. Egan was beside himself, ready to attack and destroy the ghastly rodent. Even though Genevieve knew he didn't have a chance, she opened the door, and Egan flew out, almost knocking Genevieve to her knees. The squirrel was up a nearby tree in a flash, hopping from one tree to the next with Egan running below, trying to keep up. *Smart move Genevieve,* she thought. Grabbing Egan's leash, she started running after him in her nightgown, heading further and further away from the central area.

Finally catching up to Egan, Genevieve reached down to attach his leash when she saw Teddy. He was working with a few other people in a large garden. To her right, there was a large chicken coop with a loud clatter coming from it. Genevieve hoped Teddy hadn't noticed her and tried to pull Egan quietly away, but now spying all the noisy poultry, Egan pulled relentlessly at the leash and barked even louder, getting the attention of everyone around. Horrified, Genevieve struggled in vain to control her dog. She watched as Teddy came running over.

"Can I assist ye, Miss?"

Yelling over Egan's bark, Genevieve hollered, "I could use a little help I guess. It looks like my dog wants chicken for breakfast!"

Watching as Teddy moved over to assist, Genevieve felt it was time to shed the generic term, even if it was sweet. "By the way, my name is Genevieve." Teddy took the leash firmly and lured Egan away from the chicken coop with a few scones he had in his jacket pocket. Genevieve and Teddy exchanged several glances as they started back toward the cottage, but Genevieve couldn't come up with anything to say that didn't sound totally inane, so they walked a short distance in silence.

Finally, Teddy inquired, "Genevieve, what is your dog's name?"

Relaxing a bit, she replied, "Egan. I named him Egan after a close friend who lives far away."

Teddy smiled and nodded. Staring at Teddy as they walked, Genevieve didn't notice an exposed tree root in her path and tripped, falling flat. Too embarrassed to move, she froze. Egan walked up and licked her entire face with one swoop. "Genevieve, let me help ye up!" Teddy said, reaching down and lifting her up with ease.

Genevieve was surprised that Teddy didn't have a smile on his face but actually looked worried. It was a distinct difference from the boys she knew back in the states. Not that they were uncivilized of course, but maybe missed a little compassion. For, Genevieve wasn't ever one to shy away from challenges, and that meant trips and falls were occasionally experienced. Even *if* one of her friends did come to her aid, there was usually a smile attached with little or no concern for any scrap or cut that may have resulted.

"I'm fine. I do this all the time." She said non-nonchalantly. Then, realizing how bad that must have sounded she looked to see Teddy's reaction, but there was none.

"Genevieve, what are your plans for today?" Teddy asked, looking straight ahead as they walked.

"We're planning to see the Bamburgh Castle today and spend some time on the beach," Genevieve responded. "I have never seen a castle before," she continued. Teddy looked disappointed. "Are you working today Teddy?" Genevieve asked, hoping he'd say no so she could invite him to come along.

"I'm still on standby through today. Maybe I'll see ye when ye get back. The castle is quite brilliant. I'm sure ye will enjoy the tour but beware of the ancient well in the Keep. Long ago a witch was turned into an ugly paddock, I mean toad, and now lives deep in the well, coming out only to prey on bonny young maidens like ye." All Genevieve focused on was the part about beautiful maiden...like her! *Even after all that has happened, he thinks I'm beautiful.* Then, as she looked down, she realized she was still in her nightgown.

The day should have been incredible and would have been if Genevieve didn't have Teddy heavily on her mind. The grand castle *was* brilliant, and Genevieve kept her distance from the well, knowing of course, it was just a silly tale. Still, it looked rather scary.

After the tour, Uncle Steven and Geoffrey met up with everyone for lunch. They had changed out of their business clothes and brought Egan with them so the dog could run and get some exercise on the beach.

It was a beautiful day. The sea air was misty cool. While Genevieve agreed to keep an eye on Egan as he spent most the afternoon chasing seagulls, waves and just about anything else he saw moving, Tess, Geoffrey, Uncle Steven, and Aunt Melinda spent the afternoon building a grand sand castle that had a striking resemblance to the Bamburgh Castle. The finishing touches were about in place as the evening tide started to roll in.

Genevieve was sitting on the sand nearby, with her eyes closed, listening to the mesmerizing sound of the crashing waves. As she held her head upward, the light ocean breeze moved over her body like a soothing fan, allowing the late afternoon sun its brilliance, without the burn. Egan had finally run out of energy and was resting on the ocean-side of the sand castle when a sudden wave crept up and hit him. He leaped backward, falling squarely on top of the sandy sculpture, shooting water and sand everywhere. As everyone stood up to shake themselves off, Genevieve eagerly said, "I'd say it's time to get back to the Wainsworth Estate."

CHAPTER 12

SOMETHING HAS BEGUN

GENEVIEVE LOOKED AROUND as she walked with her family through the lobby of Wainsworth Estate, to see if Teddy might be there. She saw his father working behind the large desk, glancing up as everyone walked by with a smile and a nod, but no sign of Teddy anywhere.

Back at the cottage, everyone took turns cleaning up before heading back to the hall for dinner. While Aunt Melinda, being last, finished up in the bathroom, Genevieve lay on the bed. Tess was standing at a mirror, brushing her hair with a big frown on her face. She had tried to get Genevieve to fix her hair, but Genevieve insisted her sister was quite able to do it herself.

As Genevieve stared at the ceiling, her thoughts were back on Teddy. There was just something about him that was different from anyone she had ever known. *Is it his blue eyes? Perhaps it is his deep-set dimples or shy yet somewhat flirty way of looking at me. Then again, it might be the exotic Scottish accent or his low voice which sounds so mature,* she thought. Then feelings of vulnerability arose. *Is he thinking about me too? He probably has a girlfriend and is just being nice.*

Back home, Genevieve had a great group of friends she spent time with at equestrian events as well as good friends, both guys and girls from school. Plenty of young men had asked Genevieve out in the past year alone, but she only agreed to date a few times and nothing ever developed from any of them. It seemed strange now, to be so drawn to Teddy, and so quickly. Genevieve always thought eventually she would see her friend Egan again. Although they had only been childhood friends, he was the closest male friend she had ever known; still keeping in contact with him as much as she could.

Now, the only thing Genevieve wanted to do was to find Teddy.

When everyone was ready, they headed to the hall. Genevieve chose to wear the prettiest summer dress she had. The warm breeze felt good on her exposed shoulders. Every breath seemed to draw in different aromas as Genevieve strolled along the walkway; from the fragrant flowers, abundant everywhere to the pungent sea air. Soon, the smoky, rich odor of Cedarwood, burning in the hall fireplace insinuated its way into her senses. By the time the five of them entered the dining room, the overwhelming smell of heavenly food made Genevieve's stomach growl.

Dinner, once again, was scrumptious and very filling. As everyone was finishing dessert, Genevieve excused herself to go to the restroom. As she entered the main hall area, there was Teddy, standing by his father at the desk. Genevieve's heart skipped a beat. Not expecting at this point to see him, she couldn't help but flash a huge grin when their eyes met. Teddy smiled back. Pausing, Genevieve didn't know if she should walk over and say "Hi" to him or continue on, but feeling awkward, especially with his father standing next to him, Genevieve walked past them and down the hall to the restroom. After using the facilities, Genevieve stood for several minutes staring at herself in the mirror. There was a perplexed expression in her green eyes. Digging through her purse she began brushing her long dark hair, wondering what to do next. *I've wanted to see him all day. Now, here he is, and I don't know what to do! Will he think it inappropriate if I stop and talk to him? What will his father think? I wish I knew what to do.*

Deciding she better get moving she opened the door. As she stepped out, Genevieve let out a startled scream as she ran smack into Teddy who was waiting outside for her.

"I'm sorry, Genevieve," Teddy apologized. "I had hoped to see ye today and knew ye would probably come here for dinner. Ye must think I'm dafty, I apologize." With that, Teddy quickly started to walk away.

"NO!" Genevieve heard herself yell, even though she had no idea what dafty meant. "I mean, no, I don't think your dafty at all. I had hoped to see you today too." Unfamiliar emotions swirled around her as Teddy then turned and slowly started to walk back toward her. As Genevieve watched him, she just knew he must be able to see her heart beating out of her chest.

Standing close, Teddy asked, "Did ye see the ugly toad today?"

Taking a deep breath, Genevieve smiled, "Yes, and I saved all the bonny young maidens by stomping on her when she came to prey on me."

Teddy grinned. "I knew ye were a special lass."

Then reaching out, Genevieve watched as his finger barely brushed against hers.

"What are ye doing tomorrow?" He asked.

Still looking down, she said, "Geoffrey was going to take my Aunt Melinda, Tess and me into London." She paused, "But, I think I may be feeling ill tomorrow."

As Genevieve lifted her eyes to meet Teddy's, she thought he was going to kiss her, but instead, he reached up and gently brushed a strand of hair from her face and said, "Try not to be too ill, I have a special place I'd like ye to see. I'll check on ye tomorrow then."

Genevieve smiled and nodded. "I better get back" she murmured, and took off ahead of Teddy, back through the main lobby.

Genevieve kept wanting to turn around, wondering if he might be watching her. As she reached the end of the room and turned toward the dining room, she glanced back and felt her heart jump once again, as his gaze was steadfast upon her.

CHAPTER 13

LOVE

IT WASN'T THAT much of a stretch to say she was sick, as Genevieve actually felt slightly nauseous with anticipation. Although she could tell Aunt Melinda had her suspicions, Genevieve was allowed to stay behind. "I'll have someone come by with some breakfast for you Genevieve. When they get here, order some lunch for yourself as well. Uncle Steven is in negotiations all day today, and Geoffrey will be with Tess and me. Are you sure you'll be okay alone?" Aunt Melinda asked with a raised eyebrow.

Curling up in her bed Genevieve said, "Yes, I'm sure. I'll be eighteen in two months, remember?"

With London being three hours each way, Genevieve knew she had the day free to do whatever it was Teddy was planning. Just before 9:00 a.m., Jake the porter came by with a breakfast tray. Genevieve thanked him and before closing the door, looked around, no sign of Teddy. *What if he never shows up?* she thought. Genevieve closed the door and put the tray on the table. The enticing smell of bacon and toast got her attention and before she knew it, the food was all but gone, and still, no Teddy.

Seeing the Geordie Dictionary lying on the table, Genevieve looked up the word dafty. *It means silly fool. Well, maybe we both are a bit dafty then!* Genevieve smiled. Although Teddy had an excellent grasp of how those in the U.S. spoke, he still would throw in a word or phrase that had Genevieve puzzled. Just before 10:00 a.m. she heard a thump on the outside wall. Opening the door, there Teddy stood, straddling a bicycle with another leaning against the cottage wall.

"You *can* ride a bike, aye? Teddy questioned.

"I can ride a bike, a horse, even rode a unicycle once!" Genevieve bragged.

"Well, brilliant! Howay, I mean, come on then!"

Genevieve grabbed a light jacket and tied it around her waist. "Where are we going?" She asked.

Teddy was already moving down the pathway, "You'll see, come on!"

Genevieve rode alongside Teddy as they made their way up and down the quaint streets of Bamburgh. As they peddled leisurely along the picturesque landscape, they talked about their families, friends, likes and dislikes as well as finding out they both enjoyed riding horses. Genevieve felt such ease with Teddy. Like they had known each other forever, instead of just two days.

Turning onto a narrowing path with a slight incline, they soon were surrounded by high green grass. At that point, Teddy stopped with Genevieve coming to a halt right behind him. "From here we have to walk," Teddy instructed. They dropped their bikes and walked upward through the grass for several hundred feet, then a clearing opened up. Below them, a coastal expanse so clear Genevieve was able, not only to see the Bamburgh Castle but another one as well. The day was perfect. People below were enjoying time on the beach as the waves made their eternal dance back and forth. Teddy took Genevieve's hand and walked over to a huge, flat rock where they sat taking in their surroundings. "I come up here a lot," Teddy said. "When I look oot at all this, the trouble in the world ceases to exist, and I know how loved we all are. For why would anything so incredible be given to us otherwise? I listen to people complain aboot the *tiniest* things when they've been given a world of treasures, just like this they could focus on." Teddy sat silent for a moment, "I just wanted ye to see this and, maybe, see what I see."

Looking out over the ocean, Genevieve said, "When I was younger there was a place I went also. My life was much different then, and often lonely. There were magnificent fields of wildflowers near my home. I would sit in them for hours and always feel better afterward."

Genevieve now understood what drew her to Teddy. Beyond the obvious physical attraction, his words stirred something within her, which until now had not been clearly defined. She had always seen the spiritual perfection of nature whether it was a delicate flower or the tiniest hummingbird, but she was never able to put it into words like Teddy had just done. Just as there was a reason for the beauty of nature, Genevieve knew, there was a reason she found Teddy. Tears welled up in Genevieve's eyes, "So, yes... I see what you see." Teddy turned her face toward him as a tear ran down Genevieve's cheek. Leaning over Teddy kissed the tear away, then gently kissed Genevieve's lips. Genevieve kissed Teddy back with a passion that was finally released. They both wanted more, an instinctive hunger pulling them together.

Genevieve moved down to the grass, as Teddy followed. A drumming, pounding urge was driving Genevieve as she kissed Teddy. The momentum felt unstoppable. Genevieve understood where it was all going, but it was so much more than sex to her.

As Genevieve reached to unbutton her shirt, Teddy put his hand over hers. "This wasn't why I brought ye here Genevieve. I didn't mean for it to go this far."

Genevieve didn't move, saying, "I know you didn't. But that's what makes me want you more. I've never met anyone like you, Teddy. Everything feels so right with you. This will be my first time and all I know, is that I want to be with you, now."

She unbuttoned the top button of her shirt when Teddy said, "Genevieve, ye may think this is something I've done a lot, but I haven't. There was a lass that I met last year in school. We went out a few times and one night things got carried away. It nivvor felt right. I think we both sensed it and soon affta broke it off.

"It's strange, because I hardly know ye, but I've nivvor had the feelings that I have now, for ye. I want it to be special. It should be special, not here, not this way. You should think aboot it. Let's go back, and if ye still feel the same, I know where we can be alone."

Teddy helped Genevieve up and held her hand as they headed back toward the bikes. The ride home seemed impossibly long as both were much quieter than the journey over. Genevieve still wanted Teddy, but having this time gave her time to think. It was almost 2:30 p.m. by the time they arrived back. Teddy led Genevieve toward the back of the property where there was an old abandoned stable. Parking their bikes outside, Teddy held Genevieve's hand and took her to a room at the rear. It was a very small space which only had a bed and small table with a lamp.

"It was used for the groom or stable boy," Teddy said.

"Yes," Genevieve said, giving a knowing smile. As she stared inside the small room, she could feel Teddy watching her; waiting to see if she had changed her mind.

When Genevieve stepped inside the room Teddy said, "Stay here, I will be right back," A minute later, he was back with a large blanket. Closing the door behind him, he spread the blanket over the mattress and turned on the lamp, casting a warm glow. Moving Genevieve close to him, Teddy whispered, "What say ye Miss?" Genevieve knew logically it was insane. Teddy was almost a stranger, yet just the fact he gave her this time to back out showed how much he cared about her. All she knew was, however short their time had been together, she had fallen in love.

Genevieve, again reached to unbutton her shirt as she watched Teddy. They came together, this time without hesitation; both moving slowly, watching each other's reaction as a new world of intimacy opened up to them.

CHAPTER 14

﹏﹏ ❧✦☙ ﹏﹏

SURPRISES ALL AROUND

TEDDY GAVE GENEVIEVE one last kiss before she headed back to her cottage. It was late afternoon, and she hoped no one had returned yet. The deep connection Genevieve and Teddy had was undeniable, and the expression of those feelings were everything Genevieve could have hoped for. It felt to Genevieve that angels had conspired to bring her the one person she now realized she had been looking for. Now that they were together, Genevieve could not imagine being without him.

As she walked back, Genevieve's thoughts were fragmented between feeling the happiest she'd ever been and worried about everything else. *How can we be together? We live so far apart. Why did I let myself fall for him knowing that?* The next moment smiling, as she remembered the tenderness Teddy expressed; making sure she knew he would stop with just a word. *I...we should have thought to take some precaution,* Genevieve realized. Before she knew it, she was outside the cottage. No one was there yet. *What should I tell Uncle Steven and Aunt Melinda? Will they love Teddy like I do? Seven weeks left to figure things out. God, I love him!*

When the family returned, Genevieve told them that Teddy had stopped by to see how she was. She continued by saying they spent part of the day together and got to know each other better. Then Genevieve asked if it was alright if they spent some time together as Teddy was the kindest guy she had ever met. Aunt Melinda and Uncle Steven looked at each other as if they already knew.

Tess walked over to Genevieve and peered into her eyes. "Yep, Aunt Melinda, you're right. She IS love sick, and I think it's fatal!" Then Tess backed up quickly as if it might be contagious. Genevieve rolled her eyes.

Geoffrey, who had been standing behind Genevieve, patted her on the back. "He seems like a good fella." Geoffrey was a man of few words, but it meant a lot that he approved.

The next month was a blur. Although Genevieve enjoyed time with her family, joining them often on excursions or shopping, if Teddy was free and not working, she found a way to be with him. Teddy introduced her to his mother who was the bookkeeper at Wainsworth Estate, and his sister Amelie, who was only a year younger than Genevieve. Teddy also spent many evenings with Genevieve and her family, playing board games, going to the theater or just hanging out at the cottage. There was an ease at which Teddy assimilated within the family so naturally, with no pretense on either side. Even Tess stuck to Teddy like glue when he was around.

Teddy had cleaned the small room by the stable from top to bottom and added a floor rug and clean linens, transforming it into a tiny, but cozy retreat, away from reality where Teddy and Genevieve went to explore each other's thoughts as well as bodies.

The last week before Genevieve was to return to Arizona she felt time moving faster than ever. They had visited Teddy's special place by the beach many times in the previous weeks, each filled with fun, laughter and deeper conversations of their beliefs. Genevieve had many 'aha' moments as she'd listen to Teddy talk about how things in his life always ended up much better if he focused on the good aspects instead of the bad. Genevieve's heart skipped a beat the time Teddy said, that upon reflection, he believed it was through his desire of finding someone just like Genevieve that drew the two of them together.

Yet, the latest trip had quieter moments, tinted with shades of sadness.

On the evening before Genevieve was to leave, they slipped away to be together one last time. Their lovemaking had an intense, desperate feel to it. Genevieve could feel tears welling up, knowing this was the last time she would be with Teddy. The last time to hear him laugh at her stupid jokes or see him smile that precise way that made her melt. The last time for so many things. As he moved to lay next to her, Genevieve turned away, not wanting him to see her face, then sat up, whispering "I better get back. I have a lot to pack before tomorrow."

Teddy grabbed her arm, "I want ye to know Genevieve, I love ye." Genevieve sat at the edge of the bed and started to cry.

"You don't know how much I wanted to hear those words. I had decided, if I never heard you say you loved me, I'd go back without letting you know Teddy, I'm pregnant."

Genevieve was three weeks late. Denying the possibility kept it at bay for a while, but, in these last few days, reality demanded her attention. Looking, Genevieve couldn't tell what Teddy was thinking, anxiety clenching at her chest. *Silence. I guess I know, I'm alone in this. I should never have told him.*

Pulling Genevieve back down next to him, Teddy finally spoke. "Genevieve, do ye love me?"

Genevieve blinked, puzzled by a question she thought was obvious. "Teddy, I knew I loved you the moment you picked me up after falling the day after we first arrived here. I guess I just thought you had to know. I'm so sorry I never told you." She paused, "I'm afraid Teddy. I'm afraid to tell my family I'm pregnant, but what scares me the most, Teddy, is I don't know how to leave *you*."

Teddy talked in a quiet, soothing manner. "I had wanted to tell ye I loved ye for a long time. I kept wishing you'd say it first, but I knew if I didn't say it tonight, it might nivvor be spoken, and it was important to me that ye know. The last couple of weeks I've tried to gather enough courage to talk to your uncle; to see if he would help me if I were to relocate so I could be closer to ye. But, the time nivvor seemed right. Now, this changes things. Genevieve, let's get married. I'm sure under the circumstances, he'll help me...help us."

Genevieve could feel her lip tremble. She believed Teddy loved her, and, as he always did, he was thinking about her before anything else. God, she loved him. He could have been like so many, either ignoring responsibility altogether or just agreeing to be financially bound. But even Genevieve didn't imagine he'd take the leap of marriage. They both were so young.

"You always amaze me Teddy," Genevieve said brushing her fingers along his cheek. As she touched his skin, she felt beyond any doubt, his love was as strong as hers. "It's time I care about you, as you always care about me. I can't say yes. It's not that I don't want to, in fact it's all I want. We have something I know I could never have again. But I'm afraid if we marry because we should, obligation will replace what we have now. I want you Teddy, God knows how much. But I can't say yes, not here, not this way. When it comes to marriage, it should be, must be special. I'm going to go back tomorrow, giving you time. Then, if you still feel the same…" A single tear rolled down Genevieve's face. "I'll say I love you every day of my life."

Teddy sat up now with forceful determination. "Ye can go home if ye want. It changes nothing. I won't lose ye now Genevieve. I'll just find my way to ye anyway. If waiting is what ye need, I will wait. But that baby is mine too, a part of us both. How can that not be special?"

Genevieve couldn't help but smile through her tears. "You're so stubborn," she whispered. "I don't even know what will happen when I tell my family--how they'll react."

Teddy gently placed his hand on Genevieve's abdomen. "It won't matter. Even if we have to find our own way. I will do whatever I need to, for ye, our baby…*our* family."

CHAPTER 15

꧁ꕥ꧂

SAME EVENT
A DIFFERENT CHOICE

As GENEVIEVE SAT on the steps of the open stairway, staring at the pile of luggage by the door, she had the feeling this trip would be extraordinary. They had been on many trips now, since Genevieve and Tess moved in with their Aunt and Uncle. But there was a feeling about this trip to England that was different. Maybe it had something to do her getting older, now almost eighteen, but whatever the reason, the anticipation she felt was stronger than ever before.

Every summer Aunt Melinda, Uncle Steven, Genevieve, Tess and occasionally Geoffrey, went somewhere far from home. Tess loved to say 'exotic' and Genevieve felt it was a great word for the places so different than their own. Two years ago, they all spent a couple of weeks on a yacht, stopping at several Caribbean islands. Genevieve and Tess learned to snorkel during that trip. Last year was the best yet, as they went to Africa. Genevieve had never experienced the grandeur of such amazing animals.

Their guide, Masego, was ingenious in Genevieve's eyes as well as brave and resourceful; always on the lookout for interesting sights which seem to appear out of nowhere on a daily basis. One afternoon he guided everyone to a tower of giraffes, the next, everyone was observing a mother hippopotamus wading in shallow water with her baby calf. Masego gave everyone binoculars so they could see them up close. Tess wanted to get closer to see the cute baby but Masego said there was a very good reason they were staying far away. He told of a time when he was very young and a childhood friend of his was killed by getting to close to a mother hippopotamus and her baby thinking also, there couldn't be any danger to something that seemed so innocent.

Hearing Egan, the families' golden retriever barking, Genevieve blinked the memory away and headed out to see what was going on. *I sure hope we'll have enough clothes to wear*, Genevieve thought with amusement, as a man struggled to load the copious amount of luggage on to the transport truck. Aunt Melinda never left anything to chance and so, for the past few weeks, more and more things were being packed, just in case.

The only thing Genevieve would miss was the horse she called her own, Haddie. Genevieve was becoming quite an equestrian with Haddie, a beautiful Fresian. Genevieve thought of Haddie as her best friend, never once letting her down, and always there when she needed her. As Geoffrey came around with the limo, Genevieve knew it was almost time to go and ran to the stable one last time to be with Haddie.

Sleeping most the way in the plane, Genevieve was pleasantly surprised when they were preparing to land in London. It was the long drive north, to a town called Bamburgh, located just south of the Scottish border that felt like it would never end. Although traveling in a limo was always spacious, trying to keep Egan calm after so many hours in a cage was next to impossible. He kept tripping over everyone's feet as he paced up and down the narrow floor. Aunt Melinda scolded herself for not anticipating how anxious and fearful Egan would be on the trip, swearing next time she'd make sure he was sedated for a long trip.

As they drove up the long private road to the Wainsworth Estate, Genevieve was overwhelmed as she saw the splendor of a distant past. Dripping in rich detail, from the manicured lawns and whimsical shrubbery to the pristine fountain near the entrance where a beautiful angelic woman in a flowing white marble gown held out her hand, as if guiding everyone to the large doors at the entrance.

Once inside, the females all headed to the restroom while Uncle Steven and Geoffrey tended to the check in. By the time everyone was back together, a young man, maybe a couple of years older than Genevieve, stood, ready to assist everyone to their cottage.

The bags and trunks were loaded on two large luggage carts. The porter, leading the way, pushed one, while Geoffrey followed up the rear, pushing the other. As Genevieve walked slowly down the pathway behind the porter, she couldn't help noticing his wide, strong shoulders. His dark hair was an attractive contrast to his rather light skin and bright blue eyes. He kept glancing back to look at Genevieve as they walked down an illuminated path that meandered through beautiful tall trees and fragrant flowers.

"What's your name?" Genevieve asked, breaking the silence.

Turning, the porter said, "Everyone calls me Teddy, Miss." By the time they reached the cottage, Genevieve knew a little more about Teddy and found it hard to pull her eyes away from him. His Scottish accent, dimples and just the way he looked at her, made Genevieve feel oddly vulnerable.

Glancing over at Aunt Melinda, Genevieve noticed her aunt smiling at her, and realized her interest in the porter may be more telling than she thought. Teddy pointed out where they could find extra towels and linens, welcomed them to Wainsworth Estate with a tray of hot tea and biscuits and reminding them of the dining room hours. Before he left, Teddy knelt down to pet Egan. As he stood back up, he and Genevieve held a long glance before he moved to the cottage door. Before leaving he addressed everyone by saying, "I'm here at your disposal." Then quietly closed the door behind him.

Although the men seemed oblivious to what had just happened, nothing was lost on Aunt Melinda or Tess with the comments they made. It wasn't unusual that guys came around or asked Genevieve out. What was unusual, was to see Genevieve so enchanted. For, until now, Genevieve had never shown any real interest in anyone, and Teddy was taking Genevieve by as much surprise as it was her aunt and sister.

Genevieve had always been told she had a natural beauty; with her long, dark wavy hair, striking green eyes, and a slim, poised frame. And, although thankful for God's blessing, she was uncomfortable when she was only defined by it.

On Genevieve's 17th birthday, Uncle Steven and Genevieve rode horses together--a special surprise for Genevieve as Uncle Steven was always so busy. As they rode, Genevieve asked her uncle about his life as a child, how he and Aunt Melinda met, and why he didn't become a comedian, as he always had something hilarious to say. Lifting his head upward, Uncle Steven let out an infectious chuckle. After a moment he said, "Well, trying to make a living as a comedian would be hard work I think. I love what I do, and I think I'm pretty good at it. However, when I can seal a deal with laughter, I get the best of both worlds."

The afternoon ride would have been a wonderful present in of itself, but as they brought the horses back to the stable, Uncle Steven said something that made Genevieve feel more beautiful than she ever had in her life. "Genevieve, what makes you so endearing to everyone, is your ability to make them feel important. You rarely talk about yourself, but instead, draw people out to talk about themselves. Then, you respond in ways that make them feel good. Your wonder of others and optimism about life is such a beautiful quality."

As the family left the cottage for dinner, Genevieve was thinking about what her uncle had said to her on that day and hoped if she saw Teddy again he'd see something about her that was more than skin deep.

CHAPTER 16

———— ❧❧❧ ————

A DIFFERENT KIND OF BEAUTIFUL

OH, MY GOODNESS, what is that dog barking about this early? Genevieve thought as she pulled the pillow over her head. Jet lag was in full force, and Tess and Aunt Melinda were still in a deep sleep, deaf to all around them. Getting up and walking over to Egan, Genevieve peered at the small squirrel outside the window and shook her head at the anxious dog. "You're no match, you know that, right?" Egan stood, staring at her, barking even louder. "Okay, okay." As Genevieve opened the door, however, she realized *she* was no match for Egan!

"Egan!" Genevieve yelled as she ran, trying to make sure she still had an eye on him as he chased the high-flying squirrel. Genevieve had no time to focus on where Egan was leading her until she found herself in a wide-open area at the back of the property where a large garden, fruit trees, and poultry were being tended to by staff at the estate. Dressed in nothing but a night-gown, Genevieve watched as Egan's barking got the attention of everyone. Then she noticed Teddy. "Egan, look what you've done!" she said in a hissing whisper. A moment later Teddy was there to help Genevieve get Egan under control.

As the three made their way back toward the cottage, Genevieve tried to act coy and mysterious, traits her aunt said were very appealing to men. But, the attempt fell flat, as did Genevieve when she tripped over a tree root while giving Teddy an amorous gaze. As she lay frozen and embarrassed, Egan showed his concern by giving her a slobbering lick covering her entire face. *Great,* Genevieve thought, *I'm about as coy and mysterious as my dog!* Just then, she felt herself being lifted up by Teddy with ease.

After Genevieve had assured Teddy she was all right, they continued on. While Genevieve was trying to gain some composure, Teddy blurted,

"Genevieve, what are your plans for today?" Wishing she could say she had nothing planned, she instead, laid out the schedule Aunt Melinda had made. She could see that Teddy was disappointed. Still, he amused Genevieve with a story about the Bamburgh Castle's cursed toad and bonny maidens, like her, that it preyed upon. Arriving at the cottage, Genevieve wiped wet dirt from her cheek and looked down at her filthy nightgown thinking, *Beautiful. Well, after what he saw just now, maybe he _can_ see a different kind of beautiful.*

So, the planned day went just as expected. The castle was, as Teddy described, "Brilliant." Genevieve couldn't help herself, and told Tess about the cursed toad, living in the well. When they arrived at the Keep, Tess refused to enter. Genevieve stayed behind as well, feeling a little guilty, and the well *did* have a dark eerie quality to it.

Before heading to the beach, the entire family met up at the Olde Ship for steak and ale pie. The unique atmosphere and abundance of nautical artifacts in the pub were extraordinary. Egan sat patiently outside the door, tied with a leash when the owner took pity and brought him a small feast of left-over scraps that he devoured in the blink of an eye. *What a wonderful thing to do,* Genevieve thought. Uncle Steven did as well, leaving a tip that made the owner very grateful.

As the first full day in England was winding down, Genevieve sat peacefully on a perfect sandy beach with her family working on a sandcastle nearby. Egan lay flat on his side, next to the castle, tuckered out from a full day of exercise. People had been filling the pristine area all afternoon. Although it had to be Genevieve's imagination, to her, it seemed as if everyone in the entire town stopped by to chat with them. Genevieve didn't know what she enjoyed more, their great Geordie accent or the terms she kept hearing, like telling Uncle Steven he had "bonny lasses" or pointing to the sand sculpture and saying, "Ah leik yer castle" then leaving with, "canny good taakin wi ye." Some phrases, however, were totally lost in translation. Yet, no one passed by without a wave, many stopping to admire the imposing castle.

Genevieve enjoyed just watching people, and there was an abundant supply to observe on this day. As the final touches were being made to the castle, Genevieve noticed an elderly woman walking on the footpath far behind them. The woman changed direction, leaving the dirt path and coming her way. The woman's short, ample figure moved slowly through the thick, deep sand. As she got closer a warm smile appeared upon her weathered face. Her small, triangle-shaped eyes showed wisdom, fraught by a lifetime of experiences but it was the gentleness within them that captured her very essence. Without a word, she stood for a few moments examining the sandcastle's detail. Then, with a satisfied nod, she patted Genevieve gently on the head as she moved on. Little gestures, smiling eyes, simply paradise.

But when Egan was struck by a sneaky wave, toppling him into the sandcastle, Genevieve was more than ready to head back to Wainsworth Estate, hoping she might build on something that would last a lot longer than the sandcastle did.

CHAPTER 17

SENSING CHANGE

IT WAS ALMOST 7:00 p.m. and everyone was about ready for dinner. Egan was already fed and bathed, now lying by Genevieve's bed with a lethargic look on his face. Kneeling down Genevieve kissed him on the head. "I can see why you're tired. I don't know what you *didn't* chase today!" Then stroking his head and giving him another kiss she whispered, "I'm sure glad you're here with us ole' boy." Egan licked her cheek, in agreement.

When Aunt Melinda, the last to freshen up, declared she was ready, everyone moved swiftly to the door. As it closed, Egan ran to the window and jumped up, watching everyone leave with a perplexed expression on his face. *We'll be back soon*, Genevieve thought with a slight tinge of guilt. Tess ran over to where Genevieve was and took her hand. Strolling down the walkway, Genevieve was acutely aware of her senses. The soft touch of her sister's hand, the ebb and flow of aromas moving through the silent breeze, even the nightly chatter of crickets as they charmed a mate, resonated at a deeper level than usual. Ever since she set eyes on Teddy, Genevieve's world felt more vivid somehow.

While waiting for their dinner to be served, Geoffrey talked to Uncle Steven, telling him his thoughts on the upcoming negotiations to buy some beachfront property north of town. Aunt Melinda had struck up a conversation with a woman at the next table, while Tess and another girl, sitting nearby with her parents kept exchanging glances. "Why don't you go over and say hi, Tess?" Genevieve suggested.

"Maybe later," Tess replied, then turned her sights on some bread at the table and reached for a piece. Genevieve kept looking for any sign of Teddy but finally assumed he'd called it a night. *Maybe tomorrow*, Genevieve thought.

Then dinner arrived and nothing mattered to anyone other than filling their empty bellies.

While finishing dessert, Genevieve decided to take one last look around, excusing herself to go to the restroom. As she entered the lobby area, a rush of adrenaline ran through her as she locked eyes with Teddy. *He's here!* Genevieve thought, trying to conceal her excitement. Hesitant and unprepared, she walked past Teddy and his father and continued on to the restroom.

After several minutes, staring at the mirror, unsure of how to approach Teddy, her sense of urgency gave her courage. With a determined exit from the restroom, she slammed right into Teddy who was waiting outside the door. She quickly deduced that the urgency was just as strong for him. As they talked, moving closer and closer, Genevieve could feel the pulsing rush of emotions within her. When he reached to gently move hair that had fallen in her face, all Genevieve wanted to do was kiss him, and it took all her strength not to do so. After making plans to meet the following day, Genevieve sensed there was much more than she ever imagined ahead.

Everyone was finished by the time Genevieve got back. Tess was standing next to the little girl at the nearby table, laughing and giggling. *Good girl*, Genevieve thought, proud her sister had reached out. Aunt Melinda looked at Genevieve with mock concern, "I was beginning to wonder if you'd ever come back. I noticed the cute porter was in the lobby, Teddy, right?"

Genevieve, knowing she'd have to play sick tomorrow to get out of scheduled plans replied, "Ah, yes. I saw him too, said 'Hi' on my way back. Sorry I took a while in the restroom, I'm not feeling very good. Can we head back to the cottage?" With that everyone got up and Tess said goodbye to a new friend.

CHAPTER 18

CLEARING THE FOG

GENEVIEVE HAD A genuine and open relationship with her aunt and uncle. The very day she and her sister moved in, Aunt Melinda and Uncle Steven sat the two of them down and said *nothing* was more important to them than the girls' happiness. Genevieve knew the words were primarily directed at her since Tess was too young to understand the meaning. As she listened that day, she believed it was true. Aunt Melinda told Genevieve that she would respect her feelings, stressing how important it was to talk to each other and that nothing was off limits. That's why Genevieve felt uneasy about her feigned illness. Maybe Aunt Melinda would have been just fine allowing Genevieve to spend the day with Teddy, but it was too important to take the chance.

Genevieve tried to stay busy, waiting for Teddy the following morning, but minutes felt like hours. She hoped she hadn't made a mistake, sending Aunt Melinda and Tess on their way as it was almost 10:00, and still no sign of Teddy. Then a thump hit the outside wall and both Egan and Genevieve jumped. "It's okay boy," Genevieve reassured.

Not sure what Teddy had planned, Genevieve dressed casually in deep blue Capris and a soft white knit sleeveless shirt. Upon opening the door and seeing Teddy with two bicycles, she gathered it was going to be an outdoor affair, so she grabbed her light windbreaker and gave Egan her few left-overs from breakfast to distract him as she slipped out the door.

The destination was a secret as they peddled around town. Genevieve did what was second nature--getting Teddy to open up about his life. Although Genevieve answered questions Teddy was curious about, the conversation always turned back to Teddy. By the time they arrived at their destination, Genevieve had found out his father had grown up in the United States which explained Teddy's excellent understanding of her country's dialect. His mother, who, like his father, also worked at the estate had once been a model in London when she was in her early twenties. Genevieve could hear the heartache in Teddy's voice as he described her. "My mother is still quite bonny ye know. But now, often falls into depression over the death of my older brother who died a few years back in a plane crash."

Genevieve knew all too well the helplessness Teddy felt as he spoke. "I'd like to meet her if it would be alright."

Teddy looked at her in surprise, "Okay, sure." He was quiet for a minute then said, "Aye, I think she would really like ye."

Arriving at a clearing that looked over the vast beach below them and infinite sea beyond, Genevieve felt Teddy's warm hand intertwine with hers. He led her to a large stone rock that was a perfect bench. As Teddy spoke about why he came there, and how he chose to look at the world, Genevieve understood what a soul-mate meant.

Not religious per se, but after Genevieve had come to live with her aunt and uncle, she grew to believe that there was most definitely a caring force in the universe. Soon, she imagined her life as a magnificent orchestra. The instruments were her different hopes and desires, hidden behind the curtain as they were being practiced, becoming stronger and more defined every day. Then always, without fail, the curtain lifted, revealing a breathtaking masterpiece.

That was what was unfolding now. The overwhelming feelings and sensations pulsing through Genevieve brought tears to her eyes. As Teddy held her face and kissed her, she kissed him back, her heart racing. Nothing was holding Genevieve back. Moving to the grass below, she only felt his body next to hers, his lips caressing hers, the touch of his hand sending sensual ripples that felt unstoppable. But as Genevieve was ready to take the next step, it was Teddy who stopped the momentum, giving Genevieve some time to make sure it was what she was ready for and wanted.

As Genevieve rode alongside Teddy, back to the Wainsworth Estate, she could feel the intensity dissipating; the fog making a slow retreat. Yet, the feelings she had for Teddy were never clearer. They rode toward the back of the property where an old abandoned stable sat. Leaving the bikes outside, Teddy opened the door to a small room in the rear which had a twin bed, next to a small table and lamp. Teddy looked at Genevieve to see her reaction but didn't expect to see tears welling up in her eyes. "I can find a betta place. Dafty! I know it's not what ye were expecting."

Genevieve cut him off, "No, it's nothing like that. I'm sorry I keep crying Teddy, it's not like me. I kept thinking on the way back how hard it must have been for you to hold back like you did, as it was all I wanted. But you were right. That's why I can't help but feel emotional. I wouldn't have stopped, and I certainly wouldn't have blamed you, because even now, I still want you. But I have the feeling... now, that the time isn't right. I think you felt it too and that's why you stopped when you did. I can't wait to spend more time with you Teddy, and if, and when it is the right time, we'll know."

Teddy lifted Genevieve, cradling her in his strong arms, and swung her around until they were both dizzy and laughing hysterically. "I don't know about ye, but I'm famished. If your family isn't back yet, let's go to my home, and I will fix ye some Panhaggerty." Genevieve tilted her head with a raised eyebrow, "Ah, it's a filling dish of potatoes, cheese, onions and I add some bacon for good measure," Teddy said with a wink.

CHAPTER 19

TRUSTING IN THE ORCHESTRA

As THE DAYS turned into weeks, everyone who worked at the Wainsworth Estate got to know Genevieve as she did them. It was easy to forget she was just a guest there. Teddy's mother, Ann, had an open invitation for Genevieve to dinner every night. She looked forward to talks with Genevieve as Genevieve told Ann how she had come through her own feelings of hopelessness, telling her the orchestra story among other deeper truths she believed in. Although Teddy shared many of the same beliefs and understandings Genevieve did, he hadn't been able to connect with his mother like Genevieve. As Teddy, his mother, father, and sister, Amelie engaged in the evening discussions, some relief and comfort were evident on all their faces.

But Genevieve tried to find balance with her own family as well. So, during the day, usually if Teddy was working, Genevieve went shopping or sightseeing with Tess and Aunt Melinda. Some evenings Teddy spent at the cottage, playing games or engaging Uncle Steven and Geoffrey about their real estate deals, trying to learn from the best, on how to spot a good deal and act on it.

Still, there was plenty of time Teddy and Genevieve found to be alone. Teddy had cleaned and fixed up the little room by the stable so they'd have a place they could just be together, but the privacy also made it harder and harder to show restraint.

Before Genevieve knew it, a week was all that was left, and she would be heading back to Arizona. While finishing dinner with her family, Genevieve listened to Aunt Melinda, discussing what they could to do on their final week in England. Since Scotland was less than 80 miles away, and they had yet to visit it, she and Geoffrey began mapping out the best route for a day trip. *Just one more week,* was all Genevieve could hear. Aunt Melinda had been sensitive to Genevieve's feelings, saying just the other day that it would be nice if Teddy could visit for the Christmas holidays. But Genevieve still couldn't see herself leaving him.

After everyone was back at the cottage, Genevieve said she was off to see Teddy for a while. Teddy had spent several hours tending the massive garden, gathering fresh vegetables and fruit for the kitchen staff to store for the following day. Now, he sat at home eating dinner by himself at the table. Teddy's mom greeted Genevieve with a warm smile and a kiss on the cheek. Teddy hadn't noticed her arrival, so Genevieve took a few moments just to watch him. He was so handsome yet unassuming; oblivious of what others, like she herself took notice of right away. It was one of so many things Genevieve loved about him.

Moving quietly behind Teddy, Genevieve was about to kiss the back of his neck, when he reached behind, grabbing her arm and flinging her into his lap as she screamed in surprise. "I always know when you're near me, Miss."

Genevieve brought her face close to Teddy's. "Teddy, I want to go to our room" she whispered. Teddy stared at her. Genevieve kissed him, then nodded, without saying another word.

Now with a look of anticipation, Teddy whispered back, "I've got to shower. I can meet ye there in horf an hour."

⸎

When Teddy approached, he could see light from inside the room, Genevieve was there. Opening the door, he saw that she had lit several candles and left the lamp off. She was standing next to the bed. Teddy closed the door and walked over to her. "I love ye Genevieve," Teddy whispered.

As Genevieve unbuttoned Teddy's shirt, she looked up at him. When her fingers touched his warm chest, she knew he felt it was the right time as well. "I knew I loved you, the day you lifted me up after falling. It's only gotten deeper every day and I can't...won't wait any longer. Show me how much you love me Teddy."

As he slowly undressed her, she watched his movements intently, feeling shivers running through her as his naked body moved next to hers. The time that had led to this moment brought an intense sensitivity to both of them, heightening their arousal with every touch. With precautions in place, they went well into the night, passionately exploring the intimacy they had been craving.

For the next few days, Genevieve and Teddy spent as much time as they could in their room. It was such a new and exciting dimension to their relationship. Before, Genevieve only saw time ticking away. But now, knowing all they had, she kept thinking, somehow, they'd find a way to stay together.

On the night before Genevieve was to leave, Teddy asked Genevieve to have dinner with him in the dining room. He asked chef Dominic to make all of Genevieve's favorite foods and reserved the small table in the corner so they could be away from everyone else. When Genevieve arrived, Teddy was dressed up in slacks, white shirt and tie. Genevieve was glad she had worn her prettiest dress since Teddy didn't specify it was a dress-up affair. Teddy tried not to show it, but he was acting distracted, off somehow. Genevieve had a hard time acting casual also, knowing tomorrow she would leave, and nothing looked like it was going to change that. Now, just thinking about it brought tears to her eyes.

When the meal arrived, Genevieve realized Teddy, and the chef had made sure her last night was wonderful. Chef Dominic even came by as they were finishing, making sure she approved. "It was just wonderful Dominic, as it always is. I never used to like fish until I had your special recipe of Sea Trout. If my uncle hadn't had me try a bite of his, the first week we were here, I'd never known how amazing it was." Genevieve stood up and wrapped her arms around him. Dominic showed surprise at the warm gesture, patting Genevieve awkwardly on her back. Then, thanking her, he gave both of them a broad smile and headed back to the kitchen.

When Genevieve turned back around Teddy was standing. "I guess you're ready to go?" Genevieve inquired. Teddy gave a quick smile. Genevieve still couldn't read Teddy's mood. As they left the dining room, Genevieve could see Teddy silently mouthing something to himself. "Teddy, are you okay? Not saying anything, Teddy walked Genevieve over to a beautiful wrought iron bench not far along the pathway. The night's sky was picturesque with a full moon giving off a balmy luminescence. When they sat down, Teddy wasn't looking at Genevieve, still playing out something in his head as if she wasn't even there.

Then it hit Genevieve like a massive earthquake. The reason he was acting so strange was that he was trying to find a way to end their relationship. Genevieve's heart felt like it had stopped; she could hardly breathe. *I guess this was the only way it could logically end,* Genevieve thought. She felt her lower lip tremble, tears welling up in her eyes. "Genevieve, will ye marry me?" Genevieve looked up at Teddy just as a tear rolled down her cheek. "I can't imagine what my life would be like without ye. I know it's crazy, but ever since we've met you've turned my world upside doon, and I nivvor want to go back to normal again."

Genevieve started to laugh though her tears. "You want to marry me?"

Teddy pulled her as close as physically possible, "Aye, will ye marry me Genevieve?"

Genevieve took a deep sigh of relief. "I thought you were breaking up with me."

Teddy gave her a frown, "I could nivvor imagine doing that, ever."

Genevieve felt dizzy from the roller coaster of emotions. As he held her, she knew now, that he would never have left her that way. "Oh, my Lord, yes. But I don't see how...."

Teddy interrupted. "I've been talking to your uncle, and well, your aunt and Geoffrey too. They know how I feel aboot ye Genevieve. I told them of my intentions. Your uncle asked if I would be willing to come to Arizona and he would train me--as an apprentice. I couldn't believe it. It took a little convincing for my family though. But, they love ye, so they agreed to see how it goes."

Genevieve kept shaking her head back and forth. "I never saw this coming."

Teddy kept his arms tight around her. "Well, that orchestra of yours sure did."

PART FOUR

CHOICES AT 26 YEARS OLD

BACK AT THE PARTY...

TEN MINUTES HAD passed. Rosa and Biju remained steadfast at Genevieve's side. They watched Genevieve as she seemed to continue in a dream-like state. At times, a smile would cross her face, and at others, tears were evident.

Oblivious of the condition Genevieve had fallen into, those from the party were slowly becoming aware of Genevieve and Rosa's absence. Several that had been sitting at their table felt something was amiss and started looking for them.

Genevieve continued to have the feeling of disembodiment as she moved from one reality to the next.

All of a sudden, she inhaled sharply as the next phase of her life began to unfold. An abrupt feeling of anxiety overwhelmed her. Rosa became alarmed until she saw Genevieve's breathing return to the shallow, yet consistent rhythm it had been. Genevieve had now propelled forward into her life at twenty-six.

CHAPTER 20

AGE 26
CHOICE ONE

IT HAPPENED EVER so subtly. At first, it just seemed like an unsettling change in feelings Genevieve got from time to time; something she shrugged off as inconsequential. Now, reflecting back, it had been present all along. She could remember back as far as the time her father died, and the bleak darkness she felt when she held her mother. The self-doubt and worry Aunt Melinda felt when Genevieve and Tess first arrived--then later, the confidence and love of a mother for her children. From the time Tess was little, and as she grew, Genevieve always knew when her sister was frightened, passionate, beyond the moon happy or annoyingly bored. With a lingering touch, she knew...yet she didn't.

For when Genevieve first experienced the feelings of another, she was unaware it came from them, assuming the feeling was her own, even if it was dramatically different than what she had been currently experiencing. Because, it was only when the contact was longer, that the feeling became stronger, more defined. And since the feeling never was felt suddenly, it wasn't apparent...early on.

It wasn't until Genevieve held her firstborn baby daughter for the first time that the feelings coming from Ella felt otherworldly. An abiding love, unobstructed and unfiltered yet, to protect the ego. The feelings were indescribably different from anything else Genevieve had ever experienced. That was when Genevieve understood, finally, the true and undeniable ability she had, to intimately feel what someone else felt.

But it had become a Pandora's box. Often the overwhelming negative feelings felt by others threatened to overtake Genevieve's happiness. She knew there had to be a reason for this "gift," as there *always* was a reason, but it alluded Genevieve of its purpose. Though she felt the transcending euphoria when holding her sleeping infant, people often felt violated when they found out Genevieve could feel their emotions, especially painful ones. For emotions are the most personal possession a human has, and for many, hiding them is a secret that needs to stay that way. As time went by, Genevieve found that wearing gloves, when she was away from the sanctuary of her home, gave her relief from unwanted feelings that tore at her heart.

At home, Teddy had acclimated to Genevieve's "talent," and, although it could have seemed unfair that she always knew his moods, Teddy felt it never mattered, saying, "I don't have the sense of touch that ye do, but ever since the first time my eyes met yours, I always knew how ye felt. I cannot explain it, but I just knew."

Ella was just now understanding the power of her mother's ability. Although it had always been second nature for her mother to perceive what-ever Ella was going through, it never really mattered when she was very small. But, as Ella started to expand her world outside of the home, especially after starting school, she began to get frustrated when Genevieve would ask why she was sad, anxious or disappointed. Even when Ella felt hopeful, she didn't *always* want her mom to know why.

Now that Ella was in the first grade, Genevieve knew the relationship with her daughter must be based on trust, established early, before Ella started to resent her mother for her intrusion. After talking things over with Teddy, it became a rule at the house, that if Ella or any loved one, wanted their pri-vacy, Genevieve would wear gloves. As she explained to Ella, "I can't imagine what it would be like if someone could do to me what I'm able to do with others. I believe I was blessed with this ability for a reason, and someday it will become clearer, but I trust in you, my sweet girl, and will always respect your privacy. You just have to let me know." The comforting surprise was that Ella never asked her mom to wear her gloves, so Genevieve still could feel her little girl's transparent emotions whenever they hugged. However, when Genevieve occasionally felt an emotion coming from Ella that made her wonder, she didn't pry.

Having given birth to Broc three months earlier, Genevieve was still bask-ing in her infant's perfect love. The strongest of feelings were always when her baby slept. Holding him, she felt almost addicted to the rapturous heavenly connection he still had as he smiled in his slumber, and the purest trust and adoring love for her when he was content, looking into her eyes. Even when he was tired or hungry, the feelings were always clear, simple, and uncompli-cated. By the time the baby was six months, that incredible feeling would start to fade and the more recognizable emotions humans have would replace it; the start of more complex feelings.

And life was surely complex. Genevieve did all she could, not to violate anyone's privacy without the consent or knowledge of the other, yet, in a very short time, she was going to be asked to violate her very own credo. If she didn't have borders or ethical rules to protect herself and others, where would she be headed?

As Genevieve sat at her vanity in her large bathroom, she stared into the mirror. She was twenty-six, married to the love of her life and mother to Ella and Broc. A dream life for anyone, with comfort and respectability. Yet, as she studied her reflection, the mirrored image only showed what Genevieve felt... lost.

CHAPTER 21

THE REQUEST

GENEVIEVE LEARNED FROM an early age that dwelling on what made her feel bad, only made her life worse. Aunt Melinda was instrumental in turning Genevieve's chaotic young life around by giving her the tools to stop her constant fear and worry and see life in a different way. Every night, for more than a year after she and Tess arrived at Aunt Melinda and Uncle Steven's home, Aunt Melinda would sit with Genevieve and go over her day, asking how each event made Genevieve feel. If something were bothering Genevieve, which was often, Aunt Melinda would ask her to tell a different story; one that made her feel better. "Close your eyes and tell me what happened again, but this time you are smiling by the end of it. How do you change the story, Genevieve?"

It seemed like a stupid waste of time at first, but it wasn't long before Genevieve saw herself looking at any particular obstacle that was causing distress, and finding a different perspective on it, one more positive. "Look for the good Genevieve, look for the good," she remembered hearing her aunt say over and over. It became Genevieve's mantra back then. As time went by, the clouds that always haunted Genevieve dissipated. It was a powerful understanding that had helped her countless times, when negative feelings wanted to burrow their way in and take a firm hold on her.

For the first time in a very long time, Genevieve sensed the clouds gathering again. The question was whether she could look at what lie before her and *know* what the right perspective would be.

Genevieve heard a knock at the bathroom door. "Gen, Stuart and Jennifer are here."

Genevieve got up, walked over and opened the door to see Teddy holding baby Broc as he slept. All Genevieve wanted to do at that moment was to cuddle with her baby and escape into the feeling of which she knew he was basking. But, instead, Genevieve placed her hand on Teddy's arm and gave each of them a kiss. Then, forcing a smile, she said, "I'll go talk to them." She could feel Teddy's helplessness in the situation.

"I'll put the baby doon, and meet ye in the living room." Genevieve nodded her head and started walking down the hall. When she was halfway down the large open stairway, she saw the two of them, staring up at her with an anxious, pleading expression on their faces.

Stuart Kohl had been a friend of Genevieve's ever since they were in the equestrian circuit together. He even dated her once before she had met Teddy. Staying close, Stuart went to Genevieve and Teddy's wedding, bringing along his girlfriend Jennifer, who became his wife a year later. It was a couple years later that they had little Christina, or Chrissy, who was now four years old. Although Ella was a little older than Chrissy, the two loved to play with each other when the families frequently got together.

Stuart and Jennifer knew about Genevieve's "gift," and both were fascinated by her ability. Sometimes, if they went to dinner together, Stuart or Jennifer would have fun trying to hide a particular feeling they had, and see if Genevieve could sense it. But Genevieve had become quite attuned to the nuances she felt. With practice, she had learned how to distinguish her feelings from others and could often read two and even three different feelings within another, however, she had a much clearer understanding when the feelings weren't so fragmented.

As Genevieve greeted each with a warm hug, Teddy was making his way down the stairs. "The kids are taking naps now, so we shouldn't be interrupted," he said.

When they all sat down in the comfortable, inviting living room, Jennifer started trembling with visible signs of worry. Stuart held her hand and looked at Genevieve. "Thank you, Genevieve. We know how you feel about your ability, but you are our only hope."

Genevieve looked at them and took a deep breath before she began. "When I got your call last night and rushed to the hospital, everything was so unclear and chaotic. The two of you were with Chrissy and the doctors. When I spotted Jennifer's mom, I asked her what had happened. All she could tell me was that Chrissy had been in a serious accident. It was late, and the children were terribly fussy. Teddy couldn't get away from work and so after a little while I had to leave. I hope you understand how sorry I am that I couldn't be there for you."

Jennifer shook her head. "There was nothing you could have done anyway last night. I just called because we wanted you both to know."

Genevieve then continued, "So, when you called early this morning you said I was the only one that could save her. Can you tell me now what happened? I'm not sure how I could help, but fill me in on everything you know."

Stuart was first to speak. "I understand now, when a parent says, 'It happened so fast.' You know the county carnival has been here for the last two weeks. I think you went last week, right?" Teddy nodded his head. "We took Chrissy to it last year, and she loved it. So, yesterday, after her nap, we decided to take her again this year. She was having such a good time...." Stuart stopped abruptly, fighting strong emotions that were triggered upon his reflection. Then Jennifer took over.

"We had just gotten off the merry-go-round, for the third time. Chrissy saw a man holding balloons, and before we knew it, she dashed out, toward him. She was only looking up at all the colorful balloons and didn't see the two carnival workers who were carrying a heavy steel pole, obstructing her path. It was like slow motion, watching her forehead slam into the beam, and her little body fly backward, hitting her head again, hard against the dirt pathway."

Genevieve closed her eyes. Jennifer paused for a few moments, cleared her throat, then continued, "When I ran up to her I thought she was dead. Getting her to the hospital seemed to take forever. The doctors don't have much hope. They've relieved the pressure in her skull, and she's in a coma."

Genevieve opened her eyes and took Jennifer's hand. She could feel a torrent of conflicting emotions, "So, how do you think I can help?"

Jennifer smiled for the first time, "Bring her back to us."

Genevieve instantly felt a tightening in her own chest. "How do you think I could do that, Jennifer?"

Stuart interjected, "You can feel what *she* feels, right?"

Nodding her head, Genevieve replied, "Yes, but no matter what she is feeling, I can't communicate with her."

Jennifer let go of Genevieve's hand and pulled a small plastic ring from her pocket. "She won this treasure yesterday. When I was sitting with her on the way to the hospital, I noticed it, still on her finger." Tears were appearing in everyone's eyes. "When I reached down and held her hand, you appeared in my mind, Genevieve. Of all the thoughts that had been whirling around, when I held her hand, all I saw was you, by her bedside, hands on hers. I don't know if it came from Chrissy or heaven above. You've told us there has to be a reason God gave you your ability. Maybe this is it. Maybe there is something, which even you aren't aware of, that could help my baby. Please, Genevieve at least give it a try."

Genevieve was scared. If there *was* something to whatever Jennifer experienced, then the ability Genevieve thought she had a handle on, was going to reveal more than she may be ready to know. And, if it ended up as she assumed, the best she could do for Stuart and Jennifer would be to give them some peace, yet, still break their hearts because she wasn't able to live up to their expectations.

Everyone watched in silence, as Genevieve sat with eyes downcast, moving them from side to side as if weighing the pros and cons, again in her mind. "If I were in your shoes, I would do whatever I could to help my children. Nothing would be off the table if I had the slightest glimmer of hope. So, for that reason, I will go to Chrissy. But, I still must stress, I don't see how anything I do could change what will happen, one way or the other." Jennifer lunged at Genevieve and held her tight. Stuart looked at Teddy with a smile and nod of his head. The feelings between Jennifer and Genevieve had been miles apart, but Jennifer's elation and optimism flooded over Genevieve's feelings of doubt and pessimism, so, Genevieve chose to "look for the good," and could only hope there would be some when she was done.

EXPECTATIONS UNKNOWN

TEDDY STAYED BEHIND until someone could come and stay with the children. Genevieve left for the hospital with Stuart and Jennifer. The car was quiet as they drove into town, everyone deep in their own thoughts. As Genevieve sat in the back seat, she saw Chrissy's toys scattered about, and noticed one of Chrissy's favorites, lying next to her. A tiny giraffe, maybe five of six inches tall, made of soft yellow fabric and white spots. Chrissy took it everywhere. Its face was faded and worn as she would suck on the poor giraffe's head like a pacifier when she was very little. Genevieve picked it up and held it. "I think Chrissy might be looking for her giraffe. I'll take him along with us to see her."

Jennifer looked back and saw Genevieve holding the small toy. As Jennifer stared at the giraffe, tears welled up in her eyes, "Yes, I'm sure she's missing him." The two looked at each other and smiled.

Stuart quickly took the first parking spot he could find, and they all rushed into the hospital. As they got to the second floor, where Chrissy's room was, several of the hospital staff were seen rushing around. Stuart could see where the activity was focused and started running down the hall. "Oh, no!" Jennifer shouted, and started running after Stuart with Genevieve close behind.

When they got to Chrissy's room, Stuart's parents and Jennifer's mom stood just outside. "What's happening?" Stuart asked his mom.

"She started to go into convulsions a few minutes ago! She seemed okay before that, sleeping quietly. Even the doctor said her condition seemed stable an hour ago."

Genevieve watched as two nurses and a doctor held Chrissy down while another doctor was adding something to her IV line. After a few minutes, she was lying, still. As one of the doctors continued to monitor her vital signs, the other came out to talk to everyone outside the room. "Chrissy has suffered a stroke."

Jennifer put her hand over her mouth, trying to muffle a painful wail, as her mother wrapped her arm around her. Stuart looked at the doctor, "So, what are you saying? Will she recover?"

The doctor looked at Stuart with utmost compassion in his eyes. "Mr. Kohl, I can't imagine how hard this is for you and your wife. I wish I could say yes, that she will recover, but her head injury is extensive. This stroke is another indication that without warning, a rupture has occurred, due to the trauma. If she can get past the next few days and the swelling goes down in her brain, there is a much better chance of survival. Don't give up; there *is* hope."

Stuart turned to Genevieve, "Please, go to Chrissy. If we wait any longer, it might be too late!" Stuart and Jennifer must have mentioned their hope in Genevieve because as she looked around, their family and even the doctor standing next to Stuart gave her an expectant, hopeful look.

Genevieve wished Teddy was there as she glanced down the empty hall-way. Slowly, Genevieve walked toward the little girl, as the remaining doctor and nurses left the room. Stuart and Jennifer shadowed Genevieve to the bed, while the rest of their family remained by the door. *She's just so little,* Genevieve thought. As she gazed upon the little girl that had the cutest infec-tious giggle, the abundant dark brown curls that once covered her small head were now gone, replaced with white sterile dressings. Her face was pale, fore-head badly bruised, and arms lying limp at her side. Stuart grabbed a chair that was in the corner and moved it next to the bed so Genevieve could sit. Giving a cursory smile, Genevieve sat down and stared at Chrissy's hand lying in front of her. With a deep breath, she placed the giraffe next to Chrissy, then took Chrissy's tiny hand, wrapping both of hers around it.

CHAPTER 23

THE TABLES TURNED

SHE CLOSED HER eyes to keep all distractions away. Genevieve could hear the throbbing of her heart, beating heavy in her chest. Until now, her abilities had been intimately her own, with no expectations of a particular outcome. *Everyone is expecting me to produce a miracle, but how? Is it even right to invade the feelings of someone who may be dying? What if I can't handle the pain I may feel? Calm Genevieve...look for the good in this...look for the good.* Genevieve tried to focus. As she held Chrissy's hand, trace emotions began to be felt, and Genevieve began to relax.

Surprisingly, Genevieve didn't sense any pain at all. The first thing was an intense feeling of thankfulness coming from Chrissy, not of life or even of her parents, it was personal. Chrissy felt thankful to Genevieve. Genevieve smiled, and everyone around looked at each other with hopeful anticipation. As that emotion began to fade, trust, grew stronger. Again, it was personal, directed at Genevieve. Now, Genevieve felt confident that Chrissy wasn't feeling any violation taking place.

What Genevieve did not anticipate, was the complexity, as well as clarity, in which she was receiving the emotions. They weren't simplistic, like what she would feel coming from the little one lying before her. In fact, Genevieve had never been able to read anyone's emotions as crystal clear as she was now, while Chrissy was in this unconscious state. The essence had a maturity; a much deeper understanding was being conveyed. Genevieve could only assume it was Chrissy's soul responding, and not the physical child lying before her. At that point, Genevieve's pessimistic emotions subsided, and feelings of optimism overshadowed all the rest. She wished there could be an exchange, a basic communication through emotions.

Suddenly Genevieve inhaled sharply, abruptly. The next feeling coming from Chrissy was the kind of other-worldly ecstasy she had only felt when holding an infant. Genevieve had always assumed that the only time *that* emotion could be felt, was when the Soul was still closely connected to heaven. If Chrissy had that emotion now, it could only mean one thing in Genevieve mind; that the Soul was heading home and wasn't long for this world. Genevieve felt tears building and kept her eyes closed, trying to shield what she was feeling from Stuart and Jennifer.

As her dire thoughts started to take hold, Genevieve sensed unmistakable urgency as well as frustration coming from Chrissy, as if Chrissy's soul knew what Genevieve was feeling, maybe even thinking, and sending back an emotional response. *Can she know my thoughts, my feelings?* There was an immediate reply of eagerness and enthusiasm. *Oh my God, are you actually understanding my thoughts and feelings, Chrissy?* Genevieve felt pure joy coming from within the fragile child and let out a loud, joyful laugh in response.

Jennifer could be quiet no longer. "Is she going to be okay?"

Genevieve felt strong compassion and love coming from Chrissy. Still holding tightly to Chrissy's hand, Genevieve opened her eyes, turned to Jennifer and Stuart and replied, "I don't know how, but in the state she's in, she is able to read *my* feelings, and apparently, even my thoughts, which is remarkable. I can't hear words, but she seems to be communicating by the feelings I'm getting from her. I want to try and ask her some questions. Then, maybe I'll be able to tell you more."

Jennifer nodded her head and grabbed Stuart's hand, intertwining his fingers tightly with hers. Genevieve looked toward the door and saw Teddy standing there. As was always the case, her heart skipped a beat when she saw him. Teddy winked, and they smiled at each other. Genevieve then turned back to Chrissy and closed her eyes.

Chrissy, your mommy and daddy are here next to me, and they love you very, very much. Euphoric love followed. *We all want you to come back to us. Can you open your eyes?* This time there was no feeling coming from Chrissy. After a few moments, a question appeared in Genevieve's mind. One she would never have inquired about or had even crossed her mind, yet felt compelled to ask. *Chrissy, have you accomplished what you came here to do?* The unequivocal response was of great satisfaction and contentment. As Genevieve reflected on the question being asked, she felt disoriented. *Is Chrissy's soul manipulating the questions I ask, so she can better answer them? Does this mean what I think it means?* Genevieve hoped not, and felt nothing in reply.

A new thought formed. This one shocked Genevieve to her core. *Did this accident happen so you could help me understand the full gift I was given?* An overwhelming feeling of joy and satisfaction permeated every part of her. But Genevieve's responding reaction had no joy or satisfaction. *No! That can't be true.* She began to moan and cry out loud. For anyone to sacrifice so much, just to get a message to her, was beyond Genevieve's comprehension. *I don't want you to die, please, don't die for me...please.*

Everyone in the room felt their heart sink as they observed Genevieve crying. Watching the roller coaster of emotions coming from Genevieve was too much for Jennifer, and she rushed out of the room, followed by Stuart and Jennifer's mom. Teddy moved closer to Genevieve but did not touch her. As much as he wanted to, he knew his feelings would only interfere with what she had chosen to go through. So, he stayed close, helpless, as the process continued.

The same thing kept pounding, over and over in Genevieve's head, *Why me? Why am I so important?* She wished she had Aunt Melinda to talk to at that moment, as her aunt always had a way to see a clearer, more positive perspective when Genevieve could not. There had to be a reason for all of this, and Genevieve was now beginning to realize the magnitude of its importance. If Chrissy was willing to give up everything, possibly her life just to make Genevieve aware of the full scope of her abilities, the revelation had to be worth the sacrifice as far as Chrissy's soul was concerned.

But, there was still the reason why, and Genevieve hoped there was an answer. *Can you help me understand why I was given this gift, Chrissy?* Immediate Passion, love, and eagerness were felt. But who's? The response, for the first time, seemed ambiguous and needed further clarification. *Were those the feelings coming from God when giving me this ability?* After a moment, the feeling then changed to freedom in response. Freedom? *Maybe you didn't understand the question. Were passion, love, and eagerness the feeling God had when giving me this ability?* Again, freedom was all Genevieve felt. After several moments of reflection, clarification came, *The freedom was* **mine!** *I chose this for myself, and the passion and eagerness were all mine!* Elation and joy were the undeniable feelings received.

And this ability, will it somehow help others? Again, another first for Genevieve for which she was unprepared. Instead of a singular responder, this time Genevieve received a flooding of zealous appreciation sweep through her. It definitely felt plural, as if many were responding to this question, not just Chrissy. *So, all along, my real purpose was to interpret the Soul's message of someone in a comatose state?* The feeling still felt plural, yet vague, like a weak signal of encouragement.

Then a question appeared in Genevieve's mind once again. *Can this ability also help those unable to speak, through psychological trauma or medical circumstance as well?* Genevieve was hit with such a strong reaction she gasped, leaving her chair and falling to her knees. She had never been able to feel so many strong emotions so clearly at one time. Besides love and appreciation, simultaneous enthusiasm and confidence--confidence in her--took her breath away. Always knowing there had to be a reason for the *gift*, yet never making any sense of it, Genevieve finally felt validated. A purpose, now understood, after years of tormenting questions and uncertainty.

Teddy almost grabbed Genevieve off the floor until he saw a smile on her face. Becoming aware of where she was, as the cold floor burned at her knees, Genevieve opened her eyes and glanced at Teddy who was giving her a rattled, concerned look. "I'm fine," she said.

As she got up, Teddy moved the chair closer, and she sat back down, all the while, never letting go of Chrissy's hand. Genevieve was about to close her eyes when her focus changed. She had been so wrapped up in her own self-discovery, she forgot about the small, innocent child lying before her. Within moments Genevieve emotions changed. Stroking the tiny hand she held, and squeezing her eyes tightly Genevieve pleaded, *But what about you Chrissy? I can't imagine ever allowing something to happen at the expense of another, ever! You shouldn't have to die. How can I ever reconcile with that?*

Genevieve began drifting into grief and guilt, when a new question pushed its way into her consciousness. *Do you have a choice of staying or leaving?* The feeling Genevieve received was of resounding empowerment and freedom. Genevieve opened her eyes and stared at Chrissy. *Will you stay?* Silence. Then Genevieve felt Chrissy's hand twitch, ever so slightly. Not sure if she imagined it, a moment later she felt Chrissy's fingers curl into a fist and then flatten out again, all under the cover of Genevieve's hands. Genevieve felt a tear roll down her face. *Thank you, thank you for staying little one.*

While Genevieve held Chrissy's hand a while longer, she could feel the child's emotions becoming noticeable. Struggling to stay connected to the formidable energy, Genevieve rapidly received further understandings to help her move on before it all but disappeared. Yet, even as it faded from her grasp, Genevieve knew it would always be there, *had* always been there, with unfathomable understanding and unrelenting purpose.

Finally, the familiar simple emotions of a little child were all that Genevieve could discern. As Chrissy struggled to become fully conscious, she felt disoriented and scared. But Genevieve knew Chrissy was on her way back and that her life would be vital and meaningful once again.

Standing up, Genevieve gave Chrissy a kiss on her cheek and whispered, "Don't be afraid little one, you're the bravest Soul I've ever known." After a moment to reflect, Genevieve smiled, "The *only* Soul I've ever known. You're my hero."

CHAPTER 24

BELIEVING IN THE UNBELIEVABLE

As GENEVIEVE TURNED, wiping away a lingering tear, Teddy wrapped his arms around her. His strong embrace surrounded her like a comforting, protecting vise. As he kissed the side of her head, everyone, including the two attending doctors and several nurses began to surround her.

Turning to Stuart and Jennifer, Genevieve swallowed hard, as the extraordinary interaction was still playing havoc with her emotions. Taking a deep breath and exhaling with a sigh, Genevieve assured all, "She's not going to die."

Jennifer put her hand to her mouth as tears of relief began to form in her eyes. Stuart looked upward, mouthing, "Thank you." Everyone started to hug each other. The trust they had in Genevieve's word gave her pause. She noticed that although the nurses looked hopeful, the doctors looked at each other with skepticism. *If only they understood what that little girl was capable of doing,* Genevieve mused.

A minute later Jennifer asked, "But you were crying. Why were you crying if she's going to be okay?"

Genevieve wasn't sure how she was going to answer that question. How would they feel when knowing this horrible accident was caused for Genevieve's benefit? How would any parent feel? Would they understand and accept its greater purpose? "If it's alright, I really need to go to the restroom and maybe get a little air. Then we'll all sit down and I'll tell you everything I can."

Jennifer gave Genevieve one more quick hug. "Take your time. We're not going anywhere." Stuart and their entire family surrounded Chrissy's bed. Jennifer bent down, giving Chrissy a kiss. Their daughter still showed no signs of conscious movement. Smiling, Genevieve thought to herself, *You deserve a million kisses little Christina. Who would have thought this innocent, unassuming four-year-old was destined to change my life and possibly many others through her sacrifice?*

With Teddy beside her, the two left the hospital room. "The restroom is just doon the hall, and to the right," Teddy offered.

"I don't need it," Genevieve said. "But I would like to sit outside and talk for a while. I'm not sure what to do about something I now know."

Teddy gave her a puzzled look. "Is it about Chrissy?"

Genevieve glanced over at the nurse's station and noticed a nurse who was smiling at her. Genevieve smiled back with a nod, then looked back at Teddy and replied, "Very much so."

Finding a free bench outside, the two sat down. Genevieve closed her eyes and inhaled deeply, holding it for a few seconds and letting it out slowly. The fresh air and smell of lilac nearby, brought her instantly back to sitting in the field of flowers near her home as a child. As she opened her eyes and looked around, the area was quite serene with an abundance of shade trees surrounding them. A couple sat on a nearby bench enjoying their conversation together, laughing at what each had to say. A fountain sat in the center of the grassy courtyard; a granite figure of a little girl holding her watering can. A relaxed trickling sound was heard as water dripped slowly from its spout. She wore a simple smock style dress and had bare feet. With a big smile, the little girl beamed with happiness, looking downward at whatever she was watering below.

Teddy broke the mesmerizing trance the fountain had on Genevieve when he finally spoke. "So, what was it like?"

Genevieve blinked several times but continued to stare at the fountain blankly as she recalled her experience. "It was beyond anything I've ever experienced, Teddy. It wasn't the little girl who was sending her emotions to me. I'm sure it had to be her Soul. It was a different kind of feeling; deeper, clearer, and so much more mature than anything Chrissy would be able to relay. The other extraordinary thing that I'm positive of now, is, not only was she reading *my* feelings but *knew* the questions I wanted to ask. Before long, it wasn't me, so much doing the asking to receive an emotional response, but the questions were being given *to* me to ask."

Teddy opened his eyes wide, "No way!"

Genevieve nodded, "Yes, questions I would never have thought to ask were being asked...and answered. With one of those questions I received an emotional response I'm having a hard time coming to grips with, as well as, what I should divulge to Stuart and Jennifer."

Teddy took her hand. "Keep going."

Genevieve sat for a moment replaying it in her head, then turning her gaze to the tight grip Teddy held on her fingers. "A question had formed. It was, 'Did the accident happen so you could help me understand the full gift I was given?" Genevieve then looked up, straight into Teddy's blue eyes, "The feeling Teddy, was of such joy and satisfaction." Genevieve felt her lip tremble, "You see, she suffered in such a way that she was willing to experience great harm, even ready to die, just to help me understand the scope of my abilities."

There was a long pause as Teddy was trying to catch up and make sense of it in his own mind. "But, if she's going to be okay, then maybe Stuart and Jennifer will understand."

Genevieve felt a tear about ready to leave her eye, "I said, she wouldn't die. I didn't say she'd be okay."

CHAPTER 25

WHY?

Now, LOOKING ALARMED, "What are ye saying Gen? What is it ye know?"

Teddy's reaction was nothing compared to what Stuart and Jennifer would have when Chrissy awakened. "She won't be coming back unscathed. The stroke she suffered will impair her ability to function. I don't know how severe it will be when she awakens. She wouldn't say if the damage would last for a short while or a lifetime. But what came across without any ambiguity was the feeling of contentment, even an eagerness for what lie ahead.

"When I asked if she had the choice to come back unharmed, the feeling I got was of complete freedom. I questioned, if she had the freedom to avoid such pain, why would she *choose* pain. It was so strange, because the emotion I received back was a mixture of positive expectations and an odd, giddy happiness. I swear Teddy, it felt like laughter! When I said I didn't understand the emotional response, the only thing I received back was trust and optimism. I guess she has confidence that I'll figure out why she, or anyone would choose pain if they didn't have to.

"She let me know that her choice to come back, with challenges, had a purpose of its own, unrelated to the intent behind the accident itself which was meant solely for me. I'm sure I had a pessimistic feeling when I asked, 'For whom is this heartache supposed to benefit?' There was only silence. No matter how I pressed or reworded the question she gave no reply, no emotional answer. Finally, as the silence continued, I thought to myself, *Maybe the purpose would be lost if those it were to benefit were revealed to me now.* THEN, I felt a strong, affirming trust roll through me. Making sure I understood, I asked, 'So, I just need to trust in the reason, believe in the purpose; have faith.' Again, I felt that giddy happiness. The feeling was so overwhelming

I couldn't help but laugh out loud. The last thing I felt before the emotions changed from soulful to youthful, was an abiding love and thankfulness. Can you believe that Teddy, she thanked *me*?"

Genevieve waited for a response from her husband. "What happened wasn't your fault Gen. Stuart and Jennifer should understand that."

Genevieve shook her head. "But what if it was the other way around. How would you feel if Ella was lying there, all caused to give Jennifer a message? Would you understand? Could you? And even if you could, wouldn't you resent Jennifer every time you watched Ella in her suffering? Will they believe that there was a different reason for the stroke, one that I can't even understand myself? God, I just don't know what to do. They have the right to know their daughter did the most selfless act a human could. That, through her sacrifice, I now understand why I have this ability and now can help in countless ways, those whom can't speak for themselves and need a voice."

Teddy jumped in, "Just think a little bit on what ye just said. What if it WAS the other way around then?"

At that moment, Stuart's mom rushed over. "Chrissy opened her eyes a few minutes ago. Jennifer wanted me to come and find you." Teddy and Genevieve gave each other a quick glance and followed Stuart's mother back. Teddy had made clear what Genevieve really knew all along. For her, there was no choice but full disclosure. Choosing what to say and what to hold back wasn't Genevieve's choice to make. She owed it to Christina as well as to her parents, and she would tell them all she could, no matter what the outcome.

As they entered the hospital room, a doctor and nurse were standing over Chrissy. The doctor was shining a light in her eyes, and the nurse was replacing an IV bag. Chrissy was making sounds but didn't seem to be aware of anything yet. Jennifer hurried over to Genevieve. "The doctor said it's still too soon to get an accurate diagnosis, but he thinks there are complications; that she is still in danger. Could you be wrong Genevieve? Is it possible my baby could still die?"

Genevieve could tell Jennifer was emotionally drained and exhausted. She didn't know if it was the best time to discuss everything with her, but she knew it would be worse if she let things go on, without explanation. "She won't die, trust me on that. Let's go somewhere more private, and I can tell you what I received from Chrissy."

Jennifer motioned for Stuart to follow, and the four, including Teddy, went back outside. The benches around the fountain were all empty now, and the sun was low in the sky, casting long shadows. Genevieve picked a bench facing away from the glaring sun with Stuart and Jennifer on either side. Teddy sat in close proximity to them, resting along the basin rim of the fountain.

"I always used to wonder why things happen the way they do, especially if it seemed unfair or didn't make sense to me. Why would God do that? Why?

"I'm going to tell you everything I learned from your amazing daughter. Some of it will be hard to hear. It was extremely hard for me at times. I don't have *all* the answers as to 'why' but I hope I can answer most of them. I feel it's your right, because not knowing why, is an utter feeling of helplessness; a mystery that can tear you apart."

For the next half-hour, Genevieve took Jennifer and Stuart step by step as she recalled her phenomenal interaction with their daughter's Soul.

With a deep breath, Genevieve then told them what the Soul had revealed about the purpose behind Chrissy's accident. Explaining it was with full awareness that the Soul chose to be the catalyst in which Genevieve would finally become aware of the scope of her abilities. Then, finally, telling them of the difficulties that would be ahead for their daughter. Genevieve braced for an uncertain response, pausing to give them an opportunity to absorb and react to what she just told them.

Neither blamed Genevieve or showed any anger at all. Stuart reached over and took Genevieve's hand. "First, let me say, and I think this goes for Jennifer too, we don't hold you to blame in any way for what happened. Remember, we were the ones who came to you; pleaded with you to see our daughter.

"As her father, I won't deny that it hurts deeper than anything I could have imagined, seeing Chrissy like this. Our little girl is just a babe, unaware of the wisdom and courage behind the sacrifice of which she will now bear. But, I'm also in awe of how extraordinary the circumstance is. If Chrissy had not had the accident, you would have never known what you now do. And, if you had said 'no' to us, and never held our little girl's hand, we would never know why the accident had to happen to her, forever a mystery."

Genevieve responded, "It is a revelation I'm just beginning to grasp myself. We see a child, even an infant, and are totally oblivious to the deep-seated Soul that carries the purpose of that life. I can now see, there is a purpose for *every* life. Nothing is random or accidental. Even though Chrissy's soul wouldn't tell me why she chose a difficult path to return to, please believe me that there most definitely IS a purpose, it wasn't pointless, nor did it *have* to be a complication of the accident as she had *full* freedom to choose her path forward."

Finally, Jennifer spoke softly, "So, you see, it was Chrissy who gave me that vision the night of her accident. Our little one has such faith in you. It takes my breath away to be part of her life *and* yours. Even though I know it will be difficult…" Jennifer swallowed hard, and took in a deep breath, letting it out slowly, "It will give us strength in the months or years ahead, knowing there was a purpose behind all this, and I won't have to live every day, wondering why."

CHAPTER 26

SAME EVENT
ANOTHER CHOICE

When Teddy got home, it was after midnight. He and his business partner, Sol, had been working on a business proposal to buy land, and it had to be submitted by 9:00 a.m., Saturday morning. It was an ambitious project, incorporating the natural surroundings just south of the city, into a family resort where the endangered habitat would be protected, and families could enjoy nature as well as the obvious reasons for a relaxing get-away.

When entering the bedroom, Genevieve was lying in bed, and although it was dark, he knew she was crying. Turning on the lamp next to the bed, he sat down. Taking his thumb, he reached over and wiped her wet cheek. "I'm so sorry I wasn't home when they called. Has Chrissy..."

Genevieve quickly replied, "No...at least I don't think so." Moving up to a sitting position, she continued. "I didn't stay at the hospital very long. It was so late, and the children were extremely fussy. I couldn't find a sitter, yet, I just couldn't sit at home after I got the call from Jennifer. When I got to the hospital, Stuart and Jennifer were with the doctors and Chrissy. No one, not even Jennifer's mom seemed to know much, except...it's bad Teddy. I think it's really bad. I just got home a half-hour ago and put the kids down. We'll just have to wait until morning to find out more."

After finally falling into a deep sleep after a long, fitful night, Genevieve felt a tug on the sleeve of her nightgown. Incorporating it into her dream, Genevieve was standing in a large crowd along a busy street. Everyone around was staring and frowning at her. Feeling danger and the urgent need to escape, she put her foot out to cross the street. Too late to retract, she watches in paralyzed fear as a black hearse limousine is inches from hitting her. All of a sudden, someone grabs her sleeve, pulling her back to safety. Just as Genevieve turns to see who has saved her, she hears, "Mommy!!" Genevieve wakes with a start to see Ella's face bending over, close to hers. "Mommy, it's Saturday, pancake day." Still feeling the adrenaline rush of fear tingling throughout her body, Genevieve gave her blue-eyed daughter a sleepy smile, relieved Ella was the one who saved her from her own feeling of impending doom.

What time is it? Genevieve wondered. Looking at the clock, it was 6:35 a.m. "Why aren't you asleep, Ella?"

Still inches from Genevieve's face, Ella drew a wide grin, exposing the same deep dimples her daddy had. "Because, it's pancake day!"

Genevieve rolled her eyes and smiled as she pulled the covers over her head. "I don't know what you're talking about Ella, pancake day? You must be mistaken. I don't know how to make pan cakes, only cup cakes."

Ella tried to pull the covers back down, giggling, as Genevieve tried to keep them over her head. "Make cupcakes then, Ella screamed in laughter, "That's even better!"

Slowly, Genevieve pulled the covers down and glanced over at Teddy who was watching in amusement. "I guess I walked right into that one."

Just as Genevieve was about to get up and check on Broc, the phone rang. Both Genevieve and Teddy looked at each other, afraid of what they might hear when answering it. Teddy reached over and picked up the receiver. "Hello?" Genevieve and Ella sat on the bed, watching. By what Genevieve could gather, Chrissy was still alive. After several minutes, Teddy handed the phone to Genevieve. He wants to talk to ye, Gen."

Slowly taking the receiver and holding it to her ear, "Hi, Stuart. Is Chrissy going to be okay?"

Genevieve wasn't prepared for his reply. "They think she may die, Genevieve. You're the only one who can save her."

Shaking her head, "Stuart, I don't see how..."

Stuart cut her off. "I'll explain it soon. Can Jennifer and I come over later this morning?"

Genevieve looked at Teddy, frowning, as she tried to figure out what Stuart meant by 'save her.' "Would you rather I go to the hospital and meet you there?"

There was a long pause as Genevieve waited for a response. "No. I think it would be better to go to you. She seems stable for the time being, and I think stepping away for a bit will do us some good. Can we come by around eleven?"

Genevieve had no reason to say no, but as she said, "Yes, sure, that will be alright," she instantly had an ominous feeling.

Trying to get her mind off what lie ahead and get the Saturday pancake vibe back, Genevieve went to Broc's room. He was on his tummy, head perked when he heard her walk in. His eyes lit up and his little legs kicked with anticipation. Lifting him up, she put her lips to his cheek and blew, making the funny sound Uncle Steven used to when playing with Tess as a small child. Broc had the cutest, squeaky laugh. The more she blew, the harder he laughed until he could hardly catch his breath.

Walking in, Teddy mockingly scolded, "Don't ye torture my son like that!" and grabbed Broc away from Genevieve.

Ella ran over, "You can torture me, Mommy!"

Genevieve knelt down and blew on Ella's neck as she giggled and shivered. Finally, out of breath, Genevieve stood back up. "I'll make some of those cakes we talked about if you can find some pans and cups."

Ella started to run out of the room yelling, "Okay, yeah! Then turned around with a puzzled expression, "What?"

CHAPTER 27

TIME MATTERS

It was late morning on Saturday.

Genevieve was sitting at the vanity mirror in her bathroom and observing the blank expression staring back at her. She waited. Waited for the reflection to become something more. A magic mirror with an all-knowing Genevieve who would tell her to lean close, then whisper the perfect answer quietly in her ear. But, life wasn't that easy, at least not most the time. As Genevieve moved closer to the mirror, the reflection bore the same expectant stare, as if *it* was the one waiting for Genevieve to have the answer *it* sought, a stare-off that was going nowhere.

As she continued her gaze in a paralyzed state of bewilderment, she could hear Teddy talking to Ella in Ella's bedroom, coaxing her to rest a while. Although Ella rarely took naps anymore, she had stayed up very late the night before, when Genevieve had to rush to the hospital. Knowing Teddy always had a trick up his sleeve, when a nap was crucial, Genevieve had no doubt, Ella would be sound asleep very soon.

When Ella was born, it was the first-time Genevieve saw Teddy wipe a tear from his eye, overwhelmed by the tiny perfection that he held in his strong arms. Teddy had grown up, like many, to hold back tears; to be strong, as men should be. But Genevieve knew all too well, the tenderness of his touch, the thoughtfulness in his words, and the deep emotions, always bubbling just below his manly bravado. Feelings of which only she was keenly aware.

Ten minutes later, a knock made Genevieve jump. At the door was her sleeping infant, Broc, in the arms of his daddy. "Gen, Stuart and Jennifer are here." Watching her baby for a moment, she saw the familiar smile appear on

Broc's face as he slept, knowing like no other, that heaven still held an invisible hand of love and support until he had acclimated to his surroundings and was ready to let it go. After giving each of her boys a kiss, Genevieve looked at Teddy, took a deep breath, and braved a smile, secretly hoping heaven was holding her hand as well.

She was in such a good place right now. It had taken years to find boundaries and learn how to protect herself from an ability that had no real purpose for her. Now, as Stuart and Jennifer waited downstairs, Genevieve's apprehension of what they may ask of her, was gripping tightly at her chest. It was unrealistic to think she could "save" Chrissy. But, they left their critically ill daughter just to see her, and she didn't want them to wait any longer.

"I'll put the baby doon, and meet ye in the living room." Genevieve nodded and went to greet the Kohl's who were anxiously waiting in the living room. Stuart was a longtime friend of Genevieve, and after he married Jennifer, the two couples often got together for family dinners or, the four would venture out to see a movie. Stuart and Jennifer were included among a very small circle of people who were aware of Genevieve's ability, and both were big fans, occasionally testing Genevieve's ability just for fun.

By the time Genevieve had given them a warm embrace, Teddy had joined them, and they all sat down on the couch. Genevieve apologized for her short visit at the hospital the night before and, still, not knowing the specifics, asked Stuart what had happened.

Emotions were running high as Stuart and Jennifer took turns describing Chrissy's accident at the carnival the night before. Genevieve didn't need touch to know the frantic desperation they felt. What they couldn't know was that Genevieve had similar feelings, but for very different reasons.

When they were done telling the story, with Chrissy, comatose in the hospital, Genevieve looked at them with a confused expression on her face as she questioned, "So, how do you think I can help?"

Jennifer displayed a smile for the first time, "Bring her back to us."

Genevieve shook her head, "How do you think I could do that Jennifer? I only can feel what she feels, that's all. You know that, so help me understand what you think I can do?"

Reaching into her pocket, Jennifer pulled out a tiny ring that Chrissy had won at the carnival the day before; the day their lives changed forever. As Jennifer explained about a vision she had on the way to the hospital, Genevieve could feel tears welling up, with deep compassion for parents desperate to change the dire circumstance of their child.

Yet, nothing had changed in Genevieve's mind. Her abilities had no power to save Chrissy. Was it even the right thing, to intrude like a peeping Tom into the feelings of someone who had no say, who may be dying? It would go against every rule Genevieve had established for herself. Sound rules after learning from others how betrayed they felt, even assaulted at times, by her ability.

Sure, Christina was still very young, about the same age Ella was when she began to protest the intrusion. But there was also the other rule, the one that protected Genevieve from feelings that hurt and tormented her. Feelings that, like seeing something unwanted, once it happens, you can't un-see it. When Genevieve felt, she couldn't un-feel it. Now she was being asked to feel what a comatose person feels, one in obvious pain, dying.

As everyone sat with eyes on Genevieve, waiting for an answer, she still had none. "I understand how hard this must be, and the desperation to do whatever you can, hoping it might change things. But I have to think about this. As you know, I have set in place protection, not just for me but everyone. If there was a way I could communicate, to make a difference, it might change things, but I don't have an ability like that, so I can't *save* Chrissy. I love that little girl, you know that. Just give me a little more time to think things through. It's not that I couldn't read what she's feeling, I'm sure I could, but you have to understand, it may not be something you want to know."

Stuart looked disappointed, "We knew this was a big thing to ask, and we understand." Stuart looked at Jennifer who gave a slight nod. "It was just that Jennifer felt so sure you would make a difference after she had the vision of you and Chrissy. I, myself, couldn't see how you fit into everything that has happened but felt, maybe, there were things we just had to take on faith."

Genevieve looked at Teddy. He seemed as disappointed as Stuart and Jennifer, but, it was his protective side that spoke up, "This is a harder decision than ye may think. Why don't ye go back to the hospital, be with Chrissy. Gen should have an answer for ye very soon." Then pausing, showing his deep concern, Teddy added, "Are ye still sure ye want to know what Chrissy may be feeling?"

Jennifer nodded at Teddy, then, turning back to look at Genevieve, "I'm sure this must be scary for you Genevieve. Stuart and I have always had fun, amusing ourselves with your talent in the past. I guess we never fully understood the impact it must have on you. To never know what you will encounter when you receive feelings from someone, must be frightening at times, and in Chrissy's case, to delve into the unconscious, what might you find? To answer Teddy's question, Yes, we're prepared to know. It may be the last thing we'll ever be able to know, about how she feels. No matter the outcome, we'd consider it a blessing. But Genevieve, please believe, we would never hold it against you if it is not what you choose."

It should have given Genevieve some relief to know she could let all this go and get back to her life before the accident happened. But as she stood at the door, watching Stuart and Jennifer drive down the street, Genevieve felt no peace, no relief.

After they had disappeared out of sight, Genevieve closed the door. Teddy was standing next to the couch, hands in his front pant pockets, thumbs out. She could tell by the way he was staring at her he had more to say. Walking back toward him, she coaxed, "I could see you were disappointed that I didn't have an answer for them. Is that why you're giving me that look?"

Teddy raised his eyebrows and shook his head, "I wasn't disappointed Gen. Maybe a bit surprised, however."

Genevieve narrowed her eyes, "What do you mean?"

Taking one hand out of his pocket, he started scratching the top of his head, "I think ye know, Love. Is this really how ye want to leave it? The Genevieve I know doesn't play it safe, nivvor has. It will be scary, but I don't think ye are so much afraid of Chrissy being intruded upon, as what it might do to ye!"

Genevieve fell back, flopping on the couch. "You're right. I *am* afraid, petrified actually. I can't explain it. I just know it would be entirely different than anything I've ever experienced. I can feel it in my bones. Part of me wants to know what that is, but the other says to leave it alone. What if I can't handle the emotions she has, in her painful, comatose state? Do you think there was something to Jennifer's vision?"

Teddy shrugged. "First of all, if ye handled the kind of emotions your mom had when ye were just a little lass, I think ye can handle whatever Chrissy might be experiencing now. And secondly, if there was something to what Jennifer saw in that vision, you'll nivvor know by staying here."

As Genevieve fidgeted with her fingers, she said, "You're right again. I'm sure this fear is unwarranted, and I'm letting it get out of hand and consume me. Even if Stuart and Jennifer didn't resent me for not trying, it would always tear at my heart if my ability could have given them some solace." Staring up at Teddy she whispered, "I'm really lucky to have you."

Teddy flopped down next to his wife, "Luck is accidental good fortune. What we have is anything but accidental."

Taking Teddy's hand in hers, they sat in silence for a minute, until they heard Broc starting to cry upstairs. Genevieve decided on a plan. "Let's get the kids up and eat lunch. It's 1:00 p.m. now. I hope Burt and Vi Garland, down the street, can watch them for a couple of hours. Ella has so much fun playing with their new puppy and I always feel more comfortable when they can take care of the kids."

An older couple, the Garland's lived four houses down. With their children and grandchildren living out of state, the two always seemed happy to dote on Ella and Broc as if they were their surrogate grandchildren.

By the time lunch was finished and the kids were placed in the care of the Garlands, it was almost 3:00 p.m.

CHAPTER 28

FEAR DISGUISED AS PROTECTION

ON THE WAY to the hospital, Genevieve's mind wandered until settling upon the time of her father-in-law's passing. Only three years into their marriage, Richard Walker was diagnosed with brain cancer. He had fought valiantly, but after a year, the treatments were having no effect and Teddy's mom, Ann, called to say it was time to come home and say good-bye.

By the time Genevieve and Teddy arrived in Bamburgh England, Richard had left the hospital, like many, choosing to spend what time was remaining, in the comfortable surroundings of home. The Walkers still had their residence at the Wainsworth Estate where Ann had remained as a bookkeeper. Upon entering the lobby, Genevieve and Teddy were warmly welcomed by many of the staff.

As they entered the house, Genevieve remembered the wonderful memories she had in that house, now, sadly shaded by the somber circumstance. Ann told Teddy his father had been holding on until he could see his son, one more time. As Teddy and Genevieve entered the bedroom, Richard's eyes were closed, and at first, Genevieve thought they had come too late, but Teddy's mom explained that he was sleeping. While Teddy sat on one side of the bed, Genevieve went and sat on the other. She still could vividly recall the feelings that tore at her that day as she held his hand. At that time, Genevieve was totally aware, but not skilled at navigating her ability very well. So, she allowed the torturous pain she felt to envelop her. It was not like her mother's mental anguish, but physical hurt and the insecurity of moving into the unknown, alone.

As Richard opened his eyes and focused on his son, Genevieve could feel his pain starting to dissipate. There was instead, a feeling of love and pride. Teddy kissed his father's hand, and Genevieve watched her husband as his strong demeanor began to crumble and tears filled his eyes. Although sluggish from his medication, Richard assured his son he was at peace. Soon, Genevieve felt Richards feelings being replaced with a sense of relief, quickly followed by deep longing.

That was when Richard turned and saw Genevieve. At first, he gave her a sleepy smile as she reached over and gave him a kiss on his cheek. But then, as he glanced down and saw her holding his hand, he became alarmed and quickly pulled it away, getting very agitated, saying, "She had no right!"

Teddy had talked to his parents earlier that year about the remarkable ability Genevieve had discovered. But both Teddy's mom, as well as his dad, thought it was unnatural, an evil she should not practice.

That day, Genevieve understood two vital things that needed protection from her ability: One, was protecting herself, so she wouldn't have to suffer the hellish feelings of pain when touching another who was in deep physical or mental anguish. The second, was the right to privacy for others, protection from her. It was a concept that Genevieve had never contemplated until she was asked to leave a dying man's room after innocently, and naively, receiving the intimate feelings he had for his son.

Although Genevieve made peace with her father-in-law before he died the following day, Ann asked her to wear gloves from then on, during their visit. Only Teddy's sister Amelia embraced Genevieve's gift, unafraid of what Genevieve felt, even grabbing her hand purposely, as they caught up on each other's lives.

Arriving at the hospital just after 3:30 p.m., the two maneuvered through the complex maze, finally finding Chrissy's room on the second floor. As they entered, Jennifer was crying by her daughter's bedside, as Stuart hugged his wife tightly. Stuart's parents and Jennifer's mother, all looked devastated.

Upon seeing Genevieve and Teddy, Stuart walked over and motioned them to step outside the room. Genevieve felt her heart racing, not wanting to hear what Stuart was about to disclose, but bravely asked, "What's happened, Stuart?"

Stuart shook his head, "She's had a stroke. As soon as we got back, she was going into seizures. The doctors said the trauma and swelling are keeping oxygen from areas of her brain and now a rupture has occurred. He fears more are on the way if the swelling doesn't go down soon and relieve the pressure. Why did this happen to her? What was God thinking?"

Genevieve wished she could give him the answers he sought, but it was just as much a mystery to her. Stuart, with a pleading look, asked, "Have you decided to feel what Chrissy is going through and possibly give us some answers?"

Genevieve could feel her trepidation, knowing the feelings she was about to experience would most likely haunt her the rest of her life, but, taking a deep breath she said, "If you still want this, then yes, I'll sit with Chrissy a while."

Walking back into the room, everyone had eyes on Genevieve. A nurse was changing an IV bag, as a doctor was peering into her eyes with a small flashlight. Stuart moved a chair that was sitting in the corner of the room, close to the bed. Teddy gave Genevieve a firm squeeze of her hand and a reassuring look before she sat down, staring at the helpless little girl lying before her. Bandaged, bruised and pale, there was no resemblance to the spunky beam of light that graced Genevieve's home just the week before.

After the doctor and nurse had finished their duties and walked out of the room, Genevieve took the little girl's hand.

CHAPTER 29

THE WINDOW HAS CLOSED

WHEN GENEVIEVE CLOSED her eyes, she began to feel Christina's emotions getting stronger as she held her hand tightly. The pain felt similar to her father-in-law's, yet there were distinct differences. With Richard, there was a feeling of finality, the final stages, a sort of release felt. With Chrissy, there was definite pain, physical pain beginning to be realized, but Genevieve also felt a determination; a will to live. That gave Genevieve a considerable sense of relief, and she smiled, while everyone around her watched in silent conjecture.

Genevieve wished she could talk to Chrissy, have an emotional exchange so Chrissy could feel all the love around her, but as she already knew, this was not within her scope of ability.

She kept feeling Chrissy's little hand twitch under hers. As Genevieve opened her eyes, she saw Chrissy trying to open hers. *Come on Chrissy, come on! You can do it, come back to us!* Closing her eyes again to focus without distraction, Genevieve began to feel Chrissy's confusion surface. Soon, feeling Chrissy's hand twitching again, she began sensing an excessive amount of irritation. As Genevieve opened her eyes and looked at the little girl, there was no movement yet visible to anyone around. *I just know she's conscious, wants to move, to open her eyes. I can feel her frustration.* Within moments Genevieve felt the familiar sensation that she had when Ella would run into her arms, about to cry. However, Chrissy's hurt and bewilderment felt more potent, erupting into a silent panic within her. Genevieve noticed a tear starting to fall from the side of Chrissy right eye. *I won't leave you Chrissy. You aren't alone. Feel the love in this room, fight little girl, fight!*

It was heartbreaking to know how Christina was struggling inside and there was nothing Genevieve could do. Still holding on to Chrissy's hand she turned to Stuart and Jennifer. "She wants to come back, she's trying. She has a strong will to live, but I'm feeling frustration and doubt coming from her. If you could talk to Chrissy, she's so close to opening her eyes. She wants to in the worst way. Let her know you're here, that you'll protect her and love her."

Genevieve got up and released Chrissy's hand. As Jennifer moved over and sat on the edge of the bed, she noticed the tear, still wet on Chrissy's face. Gently wiping it away from her tender, bruised face, Jennifer bent down and kissed her cheek. Staying close, she stared at her daughter while constantly wiping away tears of her own. Then, leaning over to Chrissy's ear, she started whispering, "Mommy is here baby. Please, come back to me. Don't be afraid, everything will be alright." She gave Chrissy another kiss, but still Chrissy lay motionless. Suddenly remembering, Jennifer sat upright and started to move her finger, ever so gently, up and down Chrissy's arm. It was something that had always calmed Chrissy down when she was upset, like rubbing a crocodile's tummy, it had a mesmerizing, tranquil effect on her. A technique that unfortunately had the opposite effect when Genevieve once tried it on Ella.

Everyone continued to watch for any sign that Chrissy was coming around. After about a half-hour, Stuart walked over, sat on the chair by the bed, and took Chrissy's hand. Bowing his head, he started to cry softly. Genevieve quickly ran out of the room as Teddy followed.

"I can't...," Genevieve softly murmured as Teddy wrapped her in his arms. "It's one thing to see someone like that, and feel helpless, but to also feel the agony she's going through and know there is nothing in my power to help her...it's killing me. She is conscious, yet trapped. She's fighting to live, but the pain and confusion may be too much for her to bear. I could feel her innocent bewilderment, and all I wanted was to comfort her, but couldn't. It's why I *still* feel it does no good, for anyone. How have I helped Stuart, Jennifer, or Chrissy? If she never recovers, will it give them peace? To know she felt doubt but never know why? I can't do this anymore Teddy. No matter who it is. Even if it were our own child, I wouldn't go through this torture, because they wouldn't even know I'm there with them, loving them, giving them some sort of comfort from the pain that they endure alone. Maybe that's the way it was always supposed to be. I don't know why I have this ability, but I'm sure it wasn't for this. It was never meant for this."

Letting go of Genevieve, Teddy walked over to Stuart's father and said something to him. Walking back, he took Genevieve's hand. "Let's go outside for a little while. I told Mr. Kohl to come get us if anything changed."

It was late in the afternoon. The sun was a simmering dark orange, peeking between the small grove of large shade trees within which the two found themselves. As Teddy sat down on one of the benches, Genevieve continued on, to a trickling fountain. The statue was a little girl pouring water from her watering can...happy. "Little girls should be happy," Genevieve lamented. Christina was happy when she ran toward those balloons; happy as she went around and around on the merry-go-round. What if she never knows happiness again...?" Genevieve went silent, standing transfixed and watching as each trickling drop of water melded as one, into the shallow pool below.

"Come here," Teddy said quietly. Genevieve took a seat next to him. "There are things that happen, a mystery that only God knows. This wasn't your mystery to solve Gen, and I'm sure the Kohls were glad to have ye here, even if only to let them know Chrissy is fighting and hasn't given up."

Genevieve shrugged, looking straight out, at nothing in particular, "I don't know what I was expecting. I guess I'm still trying to understand this *gift* of mine and where it is best served."

Taking Genevieve's chin in his hand and turning her face toward him, Teddy assured, "If it hasn't been revealed to ye yet, then ye must not be ready to know. When ye *are* ready, I'm sure that it will be something amazing."

Genevieve smiled at Teddy, knowing where he was going and said, "Trust the orchestra."

Teddy gave a knowing grin, "It's nivvor let ye doon before, Love."

—— ⚬⚬⟋⟍⟋⟍⟍⚬ ——

CHAPTER 30

THERE WILL STILL BE HAPPINESS

THE TIME TO gain some perspective was what Genevieve needed.

Once again Teddy was there for Genevieve, in a way no other could be. She knew her life had become much more complicated, something neither could have anticipated when they first met. But, through it all, Genevieve still felt the same fresh eagerness Teddy had for her when they made love. The same fervent passion for their life together. It scared Genevieve at times, to know she'd be the first, instead of the last to know if his feelings ever changed. But, she never had any reason for doubt. The intense feelings they had for each other only got stronger, and deeper as time went on. She just wished he could truly feel, like she, how deeply in love she was with him.

As they walked back toward the hospital, Jennifer's mom met them. "Chrissy is awake. She was crying but calmed down once she saw Jen and Stuart. The doctor said she has some paralysis on her left side. He was still doing some tests when Jennifer asked me to come get you." With that, Jennifer's mom quickly turned and rushed back with Genevieve and Teddy following right behind. When they reached the hospital room, the doctor had just begun to talk to everyone about what he had assessed so far.

"The good news is the swelling of her brain is going down, quicker than I usually see in traumas like this. The pupils of her eyes are equal and reactive, a splendid sign. The fact that she recognized her parents and was able to utter, 'Mommy,' is another very good indication of her cognizance, or ability to recognize. The more she understands her surroundings and the people she knows and loves, the better she'll be in recovering.

"However, the stroke she had earlier today, *has* caused some paralysis on her left side. Her left leg doesn't appear to have any full paralysis, but it's still too soon to see if there will be any weakness to overcome there. The most troubling area seems to be her left arm. She isn't reacting to any stimulus so far. In the next few days, we'll be doing further tests to evaluate her condition in more detail. The great news to focus on is she's doing much better than we had expected and there are good indications that, in time, and with therapy, she will be able to live a happy, full life."

Everyone's demeanor changed in a flash, as they embraced each other. Soon after, Stuart told his parents as well as Jennifer's mom to go home, and get some well-deserved rest. Christina was sleeping, still heavily sedated to relieve the pain. However, an occasional moan was heard.

As Teddy talked to Stuart outside the room, Genevieve walked over to Jennifer who was sitting by the bed, glued to her daughter's side. "She's going to be okay," Genevieve said softly.

Jennifer lifted her tear-filled eyes to meet Genevieve's. "Thank you for being here. I'm so sorry for making you go through something like this. I had no right. It was just that, at the time, it seemed you were the answer…that you alone could save her. I can't explain it. I see that I was wrong now. God, I hope you can forgive me."

"Jennifer, you did exactly what I would have done in your shoes. In fact, I probably would have insisted that you come back with me immediately to the hospital, even if I had to drag you, kicking and screaming. I'm just sorry I hesitated. Your actions only show me, more than ever before, what an amazing mother you are. Never apologize, and there is nothing to forgive." Jennifer stood up and grabbed Genevieve in a tight embrace, both struggling to hold their emotions in check.

Clearing her throat, Genevieve said, "Why don't you and Stuart go get something to eat. Teddy and I will sit with Chrissy until you come back."

Jennifer looked at her daughter who seemed to be sleeping. "I don't think I've had anything to eat all day. That sounds like a very good idea. We won't be long."

As Jennifer left the room, Genevieve stayed by the bed, watched Chrissy. She listened to the steady sound of Chrissy's heart, beating on the monitor, and felt such relief. Suddenly, Chrissy's eyes opened and focused on Genevieve.

Her gaze was gentle, yet sharp and alert. Genevieve, hoping it would be alright, took the little girl's hand in her own. Immediately, she knew Chrissy was aware of who she was by the contentment felt as Chrissy focused on her. The discomfort Christina was feeling was noticeable, but not overwhelming. As Genevieve continued to look at Chrissy, the familiar smile Genevieve worried she'd never see again, filled the little one's face. Genevieve could feel relief and an unusual giddy happiness. *You feel happy!* Genevieve thought as tears filled her eyes.

A few moments later, Chrissy was back, fast asleep.

PART FIVE

CHOICES AT 43 YEARS OLD

BACK AT THE PARTY...

A HANDFUL OF people were now watching over Genevieve as she slept. All who had attended the party were aware of her weakened condition but had hoped she would be strong enough to enjoy her birthday party. A celebration that had been long in the planning.

Twenty minutes had passed since Genevieve began her odyssey. To be able to experience the "other choice" had been extraordinary, for, it is after those critical moments that we question ourselves—our motivation, our fear. Before long, doubt is heard whispering over and over, "What if?"

As each significant choice was being explored, showing her different realities, the "what ifs" were becoming clearer--the choices more relevant to her life.

But the journey wasn't over, continuing, on an unrelenting pace. As Genevieve moves into another time in her life, she now finds herself at forty-three.

CHAPTER 31

AGE 43
CHOICE ONE

It was almost 4:00 p.m., Thursday, and Genevieve had just dropped Broc off for football practice. As she drove back home, she slowed the pace down a bit so she could savor the beautiful tree-lined streets around their residential area. Glancing at a lazy willow tree as its branches waved to her in the soft breeze, Genevieve vividly remembered the time when she was younger, at home with Aunt Melinda and Uncle Steven. The trees that populated their back yard looked similar to the ones lining the street, but for the dry Arizona climate, the weeping acacia trees were much better suited. The loose thin branches were always flawlessly manicured as was everything at the estate. On weekends family and friends would go swimming in the pool, then take refuge from the scorching summer heat under the umbrella of the inviting trees, where lounge chairs were plentiful.

Continuing on, she began to wonder, *Why don't I ever take a different way home? Teddy always takes different paths, but I always go the same way, why? Habit,* she thought. *Living on auto-pilot...again.* It was something Genevieve had become more aware of lately since Teddy had pointed it out to her the other day. She never thought much of the fact, that she ate the same breakfast every morning, went to the store at the same time every week. Even though Teddy mentioned her habits only as an observation, it had begun to bother Genevieve as she moved routinely through her days.

When Genevieve came to the next stop she got a strong urge to make a turn, veer from the usual path. *Why not?* She thought. It will be good to see some new scenery.

When she was about halfway down the road, she noticed Teddy's business partner's car parked a few houses ahead. It was hard to miss, a cherry red jeep, with a sinister looking black panther detailed on the tire cover at the back of the car. Solomon (Sol) Santoro, was the aggressive salesman in the partnership. While Teddy's robust charm and disarming dialect were usually all that was needed to seal the deal, if, on occasion, it wasn't enough, Sol would be ready, like the panther on his car, sneaky, sly, and always with a plan of attack. Teddy had started to become wary of Sol's tactics, and although usually effective, Teddy much preferred good reason over his partner's coercing methods.

As Genevieve was approaching the house, she thought he might be there on business, until she saw Sol kissing a woman by his car. Getting closer she realized the woman was actually a teenager, maybe seventeen. With noticeable surprise on Genevieve's face as she passed, Sol looked up and saw her. Driving past them and down the street, Genevieve could still see him staring at her as she peered into the rear-view mirror.

Sol was a vainly attractive man. He used to make Genevieve uncomfortable when she caught him staring at her, whether his wife, Cindy was with him or not. Long ago Genevieve had told Teddy how uneasy she was to be around Sol, explaining how, when Sol had given her a prolonged hug at dinner that particular evening, she could feel his hopefulness and unsettling lustful feelings toward her. Upon hearing that, Teddy was ready to do him harm, but Genevieve didn't want to be the cause of a rift in their successful partnership, so she said, "I think it's probably best that, when he's around, I'm not." Teddy couldn't let it go, though. Albeit, he couldn't tell Sol what he actually knew, Teddy told him he didn't appreciate the way he stared at his wife, and if he wanted to continue their partnership, Sol had better keep his eyes to himself. Sol apologized, saying he didn't mean anything by it. After that, Teddy didn't bring business or his partner around if he could help it.

Still, in all the time Teddy and Sol had been partners, Genevieve never thought Sol would stray from his wife who happened to be very attractive herself, and totally adored him.

When Genevieve pulled into her driveway and stopped the engine, she felt an uneasiness building. *Now he knows I know. What will he do? What should I do?* Genevieve sat for several minutes, trying to decide if she should say something to Teddy, or pretend she saw nothing. Finally opening the car door, and stepping out, she saw Sol pulling up at the curb. The last thing she wanted to do was have a conversation with him. Noticing Teddy's truck in the driveway, Genevieve quickly headed toward the front door, pretending she hadn't seen Sol arrive.

"Genevieve!" Sol hollered. Stopping, Genevieve rolled her eyes and turned as she saw Sol rushing up the driveway toward her.

Genevieve wasn't about to act ignorant to what she had observed. "Wow! You're really something. I guess you didn't care who might drive by and see you. I sure wish I hadn't!" Genevieve turned and started up the front steps, hoping he would just turn and leave.

"You're right. I should have been more discreet. Maybe Ted didn't tell you though, did you know that Cindy and I have separated? It's been a couple of months now."

Genevieve started to feel hurt that Teddy hadn't told her. But then, Teddy knew Genevieve wasn't interested in anything to do with Sol, and probably assumed this bit of news fit in the same category. As she turned to look at him, her demeanor stayed the same, but her tone softened a little. "No, he didn't. Was it because of that child you were just with?"

Looking down, Sol shook his head. "No, and she's not a child. She'll be twenty next week."

Genevieve gave a mocking laugh, "Do her parents know she's seeing someone who could be her father?"

As soon as Genevieve finished the sentence, she felt annoyed. Not toward Sol, well, yes toward him, but also toward herself. At first glance, it was easy to throw judgment and ridicule at Sol, feeling sure he deserved it. But it wasn't her place to do so. As Genevieve watched, Sol's typical cocky arrogance was absent. Without knowing his true feelings, she could see that he seemed almost repentant, waiting for Genevieve to say it was okay, that she understood. But she didn't.

"I know you don't like me Genevieve, so I don't think anything I say will matter. But things aren't always so black and white. Tell Ted I'll see him at the office." Genevieve felt off balance as she watched Sol get back into his car, pausing to give her a slight wave before disappearing down the road.

CHAPTER 32

LEARNING THE TRUTH, MAYBE

GENEVIEVE FOUND TEDDY upstairs in his office. The radio was playing the usual classical music that he said gave him focus. On the phone when she entered, Teddy smiled when he saw her. Walking up behind him, Genevieve wrapped her arms around his shoulders, listening to him talk to Ella.

Their daughter had always been interested in her father's work and watched him over the years take a piece of land and make magic out of it. As a child, she was gifted at art, and by the time she reached high school Ella knew she wanted a degree in architectural landscape design, so she could be a part of the magic herself. Now that she had graduated, Teddy was giving her a stab at his company's newest project. Genevieve felt the confidence and pride Teddy had as he listened to Ella's idea for transforming the newly acquired abandoned rail yard downtown into a nurturing, plant infused oasis to compliment her dad's vision of an urban hot spot; revitalizing an area that had been forgotten long ago. Genevieve missed seeing her daughter on a daily basis, but still, was glad she hadn't moved away like so many of her friends and still lived in town.

As the two were wrapping up their conversation, Teddy asked, "Gen, did ye want to say hi?"

Genevieve thought she better talk to Teddy about Sol soon before he heard what Sol had to say. Letting go of Teddy and moving around to the front of the desk Genevieve replied, "Tell her I'll give her a call tonight." Teddy looked a bit surprised as Genevieve usually took the phone away from him, even before he was finished talking with Ella. After hanging up, he could see she had something on her mind as she sat on a chair nearby.

"I saw Sol as I was coming home just now. I saw him kissing a young girl."

Teddy took in a deep breath and let it out. "He's going through some stuff, Gen. I didn't say anything because of the way ye feel aboot him. Cindy had been having an affair for quite a while. When Sol discovered what was going on, he lost it, kicked her oot. He's been doing some stupid things, including seeing that young lass. I told him it wasn't wise, that his own son was older than that girl. I don't think it means anything to him, he's just trying to fill in an empty hole right now."

Genevieve stared intently at Teddy. "*Cindy* was unfaithful? I would never have thought..."

As Genevieve trailed off, Teddy added, "Ye haven't been around them in quite a while, Love. Cindy told Sol she hadn't felt wanted by him in a very long time. That he always left her alone when they went oot, and figured he had 'others' on the side because of the way he always acted. A mutual friend of theirs, Greg, used to stop by and see her when Sol was working out of town, and well..."

Genevieve eyes, cast down, moved from side to side as she rearranged her assumptions and tried to gain a better perspective. "He saw me when I went by the two of them and followed me home. I didn't really give him a chance to explain. I was really angry, not knowing the full story." Placing both hands over her face, she moaned, "Sometimes ignorance *is* bliss. I can't leave it like this now. I've got to pick Broc up soon, but after that, will you go with me to see Sol?"

Teddy nodded. He should be home. I'll call and tell him we'll be by in a little while.

As Genevieve left the room, she had no idea what she'd say to Sol. *This was never any of my business in the first place. Why did I throw judgment around like that?* As Genevieve tried to analyze her callous behavior, she began to realize the feeling she was having was more about abandonment and the deep-seated feelings of betrayal she had as a child, resurfacing. *It's funny how I thought all that was long laid to rest, but I guess, the deeper the hurt, the more difficult to hide the scar.*

Genevieve played out different ways to apologize on her way to get Broc. Taking the same path back, Genevieve wanted to see if Sol had gone back to his young girlfriend's house, but his car wasn't there. Instead, she saw another car, another man, almost the same age as Sol entering the house. The same girl greeted him with open arms before closing the door. *What in the world! Can she be seeing two older men at one time? Does Sol have any idea? Should I let him know about this other man?* At first, she surprised herself, feeling protective for a man she had purposely avoided for years.

Then she got a sick feeling in her stomach. *Or, is there something more sordid going on. I've already stepped into a messy situation as it is. What good could come out of my meddling?* As the word 'meddling' bounced around in Genevieve's mind, it crystallized her decision. *Stay out of things that don't concern you, Genevieve. Say your apology and be on your way.* Still, she contemplated letting Teddy know what she saw so that he'd be aware if things became even weirder for his partner.

As Genevieve arrived at the football field, the team had just finished up. Broc had little to say when getting into the car. On any other day, Genevieve would have urged a conversation with him, but she could tell he was exhausted from the workout, eye's half shut. On the quiet ride back home she couldn't help but wonder about the rabbit hole she had just stumbled upon, knowing Sol had fallen down it, but just how far?

CHAPTER 33

THE DECEIT OF A LOST MAN

WHEN GENEVIEVE AND Broc got home, Teddy was sitting at the kitchen table with an odd look on his face. "Hey, Dad" was all Broc could muster on his way up the stairs to take a shower. Genevieve knew that look on her husband's face. He had it when he was totally baffled. She used to see it when he didn't understand a slang term when he first moved to the United States, and she remembered him having it often when Broc was around three-years-old. It was the time when Broc chattered on and on. Sometimes it was a meaningful conversation, but often he would talk just to hear himself speak. Genevieve affectionately called it "Broc talk"

Broc loved to tell his father jokes he made up, nonsense jokes that only Broc seemed to understand. When the joke was finished, Broc would tip his head back and laugh hysterically. While Genevieve and Ella snickered at his cuteness, Teddy would have that "look" on his face, thinking he must have missed something in translation.

That was the look Teddy had on his face now.

"Everything okay?" Genevieve asked.

Teddy looked at her with a frown. "While ye were away, I called Sol. I told him we wanted to come over and talk. I told him ye felt bad. He was so quite on the phone. I had to repeat things over and over as I wasn't sure he was hearing me. There was something odd in his voice but he agreed to see us. I think we betta go over there right now and make sure everything is alright."

Genevieve decided not to mention anything about the other man she saw and take things one step at a time. She had never been to Sol's house before which was only ten minutes away from theirs. As they turned to go down his street, police cars, a fire engine, and an ambulance were lighting up the evening sky. When they got closer to what must have been Sol's house, Teddy said, with an edge to his voice, "Oh no, this isn't good. What did he do now?" Parking the car a couple of houses down, the two hurried over.

As they approached the house, a police officer stopped them, putting his hand on Teddy's shoulder. "You can't go in there."

Teddy shook off the police officers grip, "What is going on? I'm his business partner."

The police officer paused for a moment. He glanced at the open front door, then back toward Teddy. "A call came in from someone who was walking by the house and heard a loud noise from within, thought it might be a gunshot. My partner and I were about a half-mile away and got here in a matter of minutes. The front door wasn't locked. At first glance, we weren't sure what might have happened, but it didn't take long to realize, the guy who lives here shot himself."

Genevieve gasped.

Teddy's eyes widened as he yelled, "Is he dead?"

Just then a stretcher appeared, leaving out of the front door. Genevieve and Teddy could see he was still alive. Pushing past the officer, Teddy ran over as the paramedics wheeled the stretcher to the ambulance. "Sol!" Teddy shouted.

As one paramedic opened the ambulance door, the other quickly remarked to Teddy, "He's shot in the chest, lost a lot of blood and his left lung has collapsed. Every second counts right now if he's going to make it." Teddy stepped back, and they moved an unconscious Sol onto the vehicle and were off, sirens blaring.

Teddy just stood there, even after the ambulance had disappeared. Genevieve walked over and took his hand. He continued to stare blankly down the street as Sol's neighbors stood outside their homes, watching, but no one coming over to show their concern. "Why didn't I know, Gen? I see him almost every day."

Genevieve grabbed his arm, and stood in front of him, demanding his attention. She felt his hurt and crushing guilt. "Why would you? Sol, like so many people who are deeply troubled, only let you see what they want you to see. They don't want anyone to think they are broken, even if they are crumbling inside. They give Oscar winning performances, playing a part to fool all around them. I know the self-destructive charade all too well."

Suddenly realizing he wasn't the only one left in the dark, Teddy looked around, "Leo. I have to let him know about his fatha!" Teddy headed for the house to see if Sol had his son's phone number jotted down somewhere.

When they got to the front door, he was stopped again by another police-man. "Who are you?" Teddy explained who he was and what he needed to do. The policeman let his guard down and told Teddy, "There is an envelope with your name on it, over at the desk. It probably is a suicide note. He also left one for his son. Let me see if we're done here before I let you in." The police-man walked over to a gentleman who was packing up his camera. After a few words, the officer walked back, "You can come in now."

Teddy walked over to the desk in Sol's den, the obvious place Sol had last been. The leather chair had a bullet hole which had entered the front, but no exit hole was visible on the back. The hole was just left of center which made sense since Sol was right-handed. Blood had saturated the seat and pooled, dark and sticky, on the hardwood floor below. There was no sign of a gun, so the police must have already taken it.

As difficult as it was for Genevieve to see the sight, she knew it was noth-ing compared to Teddy, who stood staring at the chair as a tear moved silently down his cheek. "I didn't even know he had a gun."

After a few moments, he looked down and saw the envelope addressed to him. Picking it up, he walked back outside with Genevieve at his side. Only a couple of law enforcement officers stayed to secure the house, but gave Teddy a little time to read the letter first. Sitting on a quaint swing that was just outside the front door, Teddy opened the letter which was addressed to "Ted"

Hey Buddy

I guess it's time for full disclosure. Wish I'd had the courage to talk to you about my personal life more, but it always felt awkward when I'd try. Lord knows you and Genevieve have something that is amazing. I thought I had that with Cindy. She was everything to me. In my mind, I still go over and over our conversation together before I made her leave, something I regretted the moment she walked out the door. I never realized she felt the way she did. How could she think I didn't love or need her? If only she had talked to me before everything fell apart.

After she was gone, all I wanted to do was hurt Greg the way he hurt me, when he seduced my wife away from me. So I did. That was who Genevieve saw today. Her name is Sheena, Greg's only daughter. She didn't know who I was when we met. Surprisingly, she seemed attracted to an older guy like me, and we started seeing each other as often as we could.

I was so proud of myself for the way I had retaliated. When I planned my attack, I thought I'd just use her for a few weeks, and then tell Greg, so he could feel the kind of pain that he had inflicted on me. But then, as time went by, I realized I was starting to care for her, even though all I still wanted was Cindy back, desperately.

Today, Sheena said she wanted me to meet her dad, said they had a close relationship and she didn't want the two of us to sneak around anymore. She said she knew he'd be happy, no matter the age difference, when he saw how much we cared for each other. She even thought it would be a great idea to double date with her father and his new girlfriend. How do you think that would go?

I didn't know what to say to her, never thought of her feelings when I started the whole stupid thing. I knew I had made a big mistake. Then Genevieve drove by. When I saw the look on her face, all I felt was disgust and self-loathing.

She's got it right. I know she thinks I'm no good and, well, I AM no good. Hold on to that woman Ted, she has great instincts, after all, she picked you, you lucky S.O.B.!

I'm sorry for what my exit will do to the business Ted, but even with that, I'm sure you'll find someone who fits in with the kind of honorable man you are. Someone that can make you proud.

Signing off,
Sol

After Teddy had read the letter, he handed it to Genevieve. Without any expression, he said, "I have to call Leo." He got back up and walked into the house. Genevieve read the letter, then read it again.

Playing things back in her mind, she realized the other man she saw earlier was Sheena's father, Greg. *She looked so happy. She probably told her father she wanted him to meet her boyfriend Sol.* Genevieve felt she might be sick. *What if I hadn't come by and seen them out front? Was I the one who sent him over the edge?*

When Teddy didn't come back out, Genevieve got up and went inside. He was sitting on the edge of the desk, looking at all the pictures and awards on the wall. There were several of Sol and Teddy at various business functions. In each, Cindy was also in the picture, displaying a happy face next to a beaming Sol. But Teddy's smile seemed slight and forced. Genevieve realized when looking at them how selfish she had been in her attempt to avoid Sol. Even though Teddy never made her feel guilty for staying behind, it had to have hurt his feelings to receive awards and accolades, always by himself.

Genevieve wrapped her arms tight around Teddy as if she would never let go as he pulled her close, burying his face in her chest. She couldn't tell if it was his, or her own acute feelings of guilt and regret that pounded at her heart like a sledgehammer. "Did you get a hold of Leo?" She asked.

Teddy lifted his eyes, those beautiful blue eyes that showed such heartache. "Aye. He's on the way to the hospital."

Genevieve nodded. "Good. We should go too. I think he'll pull through Teddy. Deep down, I don't believe he really wanted to die. He had to have known a foolproof way to get the job done if that was his true goal. He just felt utterly alone, momentarily trapped in his deception, and didn't know what else to do. I wish I hadn't seen him earlier today and said the things I said. Maybe everything would have turned out differently, it wouldn't have been the last straw, and he would have found another way to resolve things.

"But no matter, now the bandage that was hiding the festering wound is finally off. The hurt is out in the open and exposed. *Now* Sol can get help, and then he'll realize things never were as hopeless as he thought when he held that gun to his chest."

Genevieve stroked Teddy's cheek and bent down to kiss his lips. They held tight to each other for several minutes. Then before leaving, Teddy picked up the letter for Leo and put it in his pocket.

CHAPTER 34

IF ONLY

WHEN THEY ARRIVED at the emergency ward of the hospital, the nurse at the desk said that Sol had been taken up to the third floor and was in surgery. As Genevieve and Teddy rushed to the elevator, Cindy was already standing there, waiting for the doors to open. Genevieve touched her on the shoulder. When Cindy saw Genevieve, she broke down. Genevieve didn't say a word but wrapped her arms around Cindy. The deep guilt and hurt Genevieve felt from Cindy was expected. What Genevieve didn't expect was an abiding love Cindy still felt for Sol, something that surprised Genevieve after all that had happened. But then again, Cindy didn't *know* all that had happened.

When they got to the third floor, Leo was already there, pacing in the waiting room. Teddy, Genevieve, and Cindy rushed over to him. Cindy grabbed her son, and both started to cry. After a few moments, Teddy asked, "Leo do ye know what is happening?"

Leo wiped his eye, "He's still in surgery. I haven't been able to talk to anyone yet, and the nurses won't tell me anything." Looking at his mom, Leo confessed, "I haven't spoken to him in weeks, Mom. He kept acting like he was happy to be alone; free. All he wanted to do with me was go out and drink, and he drank way too much. So, I finally blew up, and since then we haven't talked. I had no idea, Mom, no idea he would do this."

Cindy's lip was trembling as she quickly absolved her son of any fault. "Don't you dare blame yourself. We all know this was because of me, because of what I did to him. I had no idea I'd destroy him like that. I never thought he cared enough or needed me. It wasn't until I left that I started to see a glimmer of the man I had fallen in love with long ago. He came by my office at work, just days after we split, apologizing for making me leave. He said he wanted me to come back, that he was lost without me. Deep down, I wanted that too. I knew Greg and I would never be able to make it work, but I also wasn't sure anything would change if I came back to Sol. After that, he sent me flowers at work a couple of times and left notes on my car door until about two weeks ago. Since then, nothing. I realized if I didn't let him know how I felt, and soon, he may finally give up me; maybe he already had. What's so ironic is that I got into a huge argument with Greg this afternoon. I told him I wanted to try and work things out with Sol. If only I had acted sooner."

The words, "If only" played over and over in Genevieve's mind. There were so many that could have made a difference. "If only" Cindy had acted earlier to let him know how she felt. "If only" Leo had been more patient with his father. "If only" Genevieve had been less judgmental..., *if only* she had stayed on her usual route home.

An hour had gone by when finally, the surgeon came out. "Are you Mr. Santoro's family?" Leo nodded. "Mr. Santoro came through surgery. He's critical but stable. The bullet went through his left lung but missed any major arteries. He had lost a lot of blood by the time he got here, but now his vitals are up and looking good. For the most part, whether he thinks so or not, he was pretty lucky. I've repaired the damage and he's resting comfortably. He's pretty sedated but it will do him good to see people who love him."

Leo shook the surgeon's hand, then followed him to the recovery room to see his dad. When Teddy got up to get a cup of coffee, Genevieve sat next to Cindy and took her hand. "Over the years, I've seen people do some crazy things when they were hurt and lost. There is no denying, Sol took it to the extreme. Before today, I didn't even know you two had separated. It was a shock when I found out. But now, after all you have said, I can see there is still hope. Tell him you want to try again, Cindy. God knows, he wants you back. I would guess it's going to take a lot of patience and understanding to feel secure again, for both of you. But don't let the "If onlys" be the end of your story together. "I'm sorry we were never closer Cindy--that I could have been someone you could have leaned on."

Cindy interjected, "I always looked forward to seeing you at the business functions, and the past couple of years there have been quite a few, grand openings, environmental awards, design awards.... Suddenly, you stopped coming to them. I wondered why, and asked Sol if you and Ted were having problems, although I couldn't imagine that being the reason. Sol just said you felt uncomfortable going to them."

Genevieve had to acknowledge. *Half the truth is better than nothing I guess. Obviously, he's not going to tell her it was he that I felt uncomfortable around.* Still, Cindy didn't need to know anything different. It had to be crystal clear to Sol now, that if he wanted his wife back, he'd have to change his behavior. Nodding her head, Genevieve replied, "Yes, the functions would bother me. I can't explain it. But I'll be coming to them from now on. It was wrong of me, not to be there to support Teddy and the impressive business the two of them have built, no matter how I felt."

Cindy smiled and tightened the squeeze on Genevieve's hand. "You and Ted have a love that is quite rare. I hope you know that. I always envied the way Ted would look at you when we were at those dinners; the way you looked at him. His attentiveness toward you, the way you held hands and whispered to each other. That's what I wish to have with Sol."

Genevieve grinned as she saw Teddy coming back toward them. "I pinch myself every day Cindy, to make sure it's not a dream, *every day.*"

Knowing that it would be awhile, Teddy, Genevieve, and Cindy went to the cafeteria to get something to eat while Leo sat with his dad. When they came back, Leo was sitting in the waiting room. Cindy became alarmed. "Why aren't you with your father? Is he alright?"

Holding his hand up, "He's fine, Mother, or will be. He knows you're here and wants to see you." Cindy grabbed Genevieve's arm and smiled. Genevieve felt strong hopefulness pulsing through Cindy and an urgency to be with him.

As Leo led his mother away, only Teddy and Genevieve were left in the waiting room. Genevieve could see the relief on her husband's face. "What are you thinking Teddy?"

He raised his eyebrows and let out a long breath, "Well, I was thinking about work. I don't think anyone needs to know what happened today. I'll do my best to protect his privacy. It will be business as usual when Sol comes back, if that is what he wants."

Genevieve gave him an assuring smile. "Business as usual. I think it will be exactly what Sol will want."

Teddy smiled back and nodded. "I think I can wait until tomorrow to see him, let Sol be with his family and get some rest tonight. I betta tell the nurse, so they won't wonder where we went. Then, I have a stop to make before we head home."

Genevieve gave him a puzzled look but shrugged her shoulders and said, "Sure, whatever you want."

Teddy drove back to Sol's house and got out. Knowing where Sol hid his house key, he took it and opened the door. Genevieve followed. She began to have an idea as to why Teddy had returned. He went to the kitchen and grabbed a large bucket under the sink and filled it with warm water. After locating some rags, brushes, bleach and cleaning detergent, he went over to the desk area, knelt down and started to clean the blood off the floor. Without looking up he commented, "I will get him a new chair tomorrow."

Genevieve's overwhelming emotions for her husband choked tight within her throat, "I'll help you," she said, as she knelt down beside him and picked up a scrub brush.

Just before they left, Teddy took the two envelopes containing the letters; the one addressed to him and the other addressed to Leo, and placed them inconspicuously back on the desk where he had found them. Looking at Genevieve, he said softly, "He'll nivvor know I read it. If he still wants me to know how he felt in that frame of mind, he can give the letter to me himself, but I don't think he will. I think he'll be relieved to see it still on the desk, his personal, agonizing thoughts still private. I'd rather he knows I can be someone he feels he can lean on now, in life, than just someone he felt he needed to confess to in death."

Genevieve nodded. "You're a very wise man, Mr. Walker."

CHAPTER 35

SAME EVENT
A DIFFERENT CHOICE

I T WAS LATE afternoon on Thursday, and Genevieve had just dropped Broc off for football practice. She found herself driving down the same residential streets she had a million times before, but, this time she gave it some thought. There were at least three other similar routes she could go, so why did she always pick this same one?

Habit, she thought. *We are such creatures of habit. Like the same people I see at the grocery store each week, same day, same time. We all live on auto-pilot, coasting through life with our same day to day routines. What would be different if I took another route home or went to the store on Wednesday night instead of Saturday morning?*

As Genevieve continued down the tree-lined streets, heading back home, she had a strong urge to change it up, take a different way home, just to be different. But then, she fought the compulsion, and chose to continue along her path, feeling comfortable in knowing what to expect. The familiarity had a soothing consistency to it, lulling the psyche into a complacent state of ordinary.

Ella had just called when Genevieve had to leave on her errand and she hoped Teddy would still be chatting with her by the time Genevieve got back, so that she could say "Hi" to her daughter. But it was very likely the conversation would still be going when she got back. These days, Genevieve had to pry the phone away from her husband to talk to Ella, as father and daughter immersed themselves in Teddy's latest development project. Just as Uncle Steven had taken Teddy under his wing long ago, now Ella needed encouragement as she made her way as an architectural landscaper. Genevieve could just see Teddy's excitement when Ella called, looking to him for advice and guidance.

As she drifted in thought, she wondered about Broc. Unlike his sister who knew what she wanted by the time she was in high school, Broc had no specific interest yet. He was tall, easy-going and handsome like his dad; quite the charmer as well. And, although he got good grades in school and enjoyed sports, playing football, baseball, and golf, he wasn't exceptional enough to be noticed, nor did he seem to care. For now, he was enjoying life, his friends... the girls. Teddy told him earlier in the year that he needed to start focusing on what he wanted for his life. But, Genevieve wasn't concerned. She loved that Broc didn't take life so seriously yet. There was plenty of time for that, and she reminded Teddy that neither of them had a plan at that age either.

Almost home, Genevieve sat, idling at a red light. Seeing her turn light change to green, she made a left turn at the intersection. As she glanced to the right, OH MY G...."

CHAPTER 36

LOOKING FOR THE RAINBOW

THREE DAYS LATER.

Where am I?

Open your eyes, Genevieve...

I'm so tired...

Why can't I open my eyes?

Oh God, my head hurts, everything hurts.

What's that sound?

Open your eyes already!!

As Genevieve willed her eyes to open, everything around her was out of focus, foreign, surreal. Slowly and painfully turning her head to one side, she saw something that made sense. *Teddy*. Sitting on a chair next to her, his eyes were closed, head tilted forward. Trying to shake the cobwebs and the strong urge to sink back into nothingness, Genevieve made her eyes open as wide as she could. *I'm in a hospital. Why?...* As the pain continued to throb, excruciatingly in her skull, she let out a moan.

Teddy jumped to attention. "Gen! Oh thank God, Gen, you're awake!" He bent down and kissed her cheek, then ran to the door and yelled, "She's awake!" Genevieve tried to keep her eyes open, but sleep won the battle.

Two hours later.

Genevieve heard muffled voices. This time she was able to open her eyes and focus quicker. Teddy still hadn't moved from her side, but now she saw her children. Ella was holding Genevieve's hand while Broc was staring out the hospital window. "Mom!" Ella whispered loudly. Broc turned and quickly moved to the bed.

Trying to find words for what Genevieve wanted to say was difficult. "What...?"

Ella finished the sentence, "Happened?" Genevieve made a slight nod, trying to keep her eyes open. "You were in an accident, Mom. A terrible accident." As Genevieve struggled to keep her eyes open, she could see Ella's lip trembling. "But, you're going to be fine now." As Genevieve squeezed Ella's hand, she watched as a tear moved down her daughter's cheek.

Genevieve tried to move, but everything hurt. She could see, and feel things attached to different parts of her body. She slowly moved her head to face Teddy and Broc. Looking at the strain in all their faces, Genevieve was beginning to grasp the severity of her situation. Speaking in a slow, methodical manner, she said, "I remember driving home, but nothing else. Tell me what happened."

Just then a doctor came in. Ella got up so he could check on Genevieve. "Good, you're awake." Genevieve tried to smile, but it was easier to stay still, so she just blinked and tried to nod.

Teddy advised the doctor, "I was just aboot to tell her what happened. She wants to know."

The doctor looked at the monitor above Genevieve's head then back down at her, "Do you need some help with the pain?"

Genevieve nodded, then uttered, "Will it put me back to sleep?"

The doctor smiled, "No, I can give you something that won't make you drowsy, if that's what you want."

Genevieve forced a small grin, "Okay then." She said. While a nurse came in and added medication to Genevieve's IV line, the doctor stood by, waiting for Teddy to tell Genevieve about her injuries, in his own way.

As Genevieve brought her focus back to Teddy, he began. "Ye had just dropped Broc off at practice. Do ye remember that?"

Genevieve squinted her eyes to see if that would help her memory. "I sort of remember."

Nodding his head, Teddy continued, "Ye were almost home. Several people witnessed the accident. They said the light had turned green and ye had the right of way. A car was going straight, from the other direction, ran the red light and hit ye, full force at almost 50 miles an hour. Your car flipped over Gen."

Genevieve closed her eyes, trying to pinpoint what hurt the most. Besides a painful headache, there was a dull ache in her mid-section, and pain in the lower part of her left leg. Her chest hurt as she tried to breath. It did no good to stay in the dark, so opening her eyes, she took a matter-of-fact attitude and asked, "So, what was the damage?"

Teddy looked at the doctor, "Doc correct me if I say something wrong." The doctor nodded. "Well, Love, ye have a pretty big cut on your head. It took fifteen stitches. Your left leg has a deep cut on your thigh and it got scrapped up pretty bad too. But Gen, your spleen was badly damaged. The doc said they tried to remove it doing a....what did ye call it doc?"

The doctor answered, "A laparoscopic splenectomy."

Teddy nodded, "Aye, because it was less invasive, smaller incision." Teddy glanced at the doctor who nodded with approval. Continuing, "But the bleeding was getting worse Gen, so they had to open ye up and take it out. They also had to remove a rib that had splintered and punctured your lung."

Genevieve looked around at all the grave faces. Even though the pain was significant, Genevieve had to be brave and take some of their worries away. "Oh, was that all? By the way you all were acting, I thought it was something serious." Ella and Broc let out a little laugh, but as she glanced at Teddy, she knew he wasn't buying her attempt at humor.

Broc walked over to his mother and gently put his arms around her. She knew her precious boy, how deep his emotions went, and could feel his anguish and misplaced guilt. Speaking just above a whisper, Genevieve said, "Oh, my sweet son, you sure feel good to me. But you know I can sense the blame you're punishing yourself with and I won't have it. How could you ever think this happened because of you? Broc, that is such a damaging emotion and farthest from the truth."

Broc muttered, "But if you hadn't driven me...."

Genevieve frowned, "Stop it, right now. I'll have you know when I was driving back home, I almost took a different way. I had thought about taking an earlier turn; to change my habit of the usual routine." Genevieve glanced at Teddy who gave her a grin and a nod. "But then, the routine won out, habits are hard to change, so I didn't change course. If I had, none of this would have happened. Still, I don't blame myself either. What good would it do now? The only thing we can ever do is move forward and...?"

Broc and Ella both chimed in, "Look for the good."

Genevieve slowly blinked in acknowledgment. "So, here's what is good: I'm alive. The injuries will heal. I get to have my family dote on me for a while, and, very important...I've learned it's good to pay attention when something inside says, turn!" Broc smiled, and the expression on his face slowly changed to relief.

When she had finished, the doctor advised he needed to check on Genevieve's incisions. Everyone but Teddy left the room. As the doctor lifted Genevieve's gown, she saw the dark purple bruises, the cuts, and scrapes covering much of her body. There was a bandage on her left thigh as well as bandages on her upper abdomen and lower left rib cage. As the doctor peeled the bandages away, Genevieve felt like she was looking at someone else. The impact of seeing the damage to her body made her feel ill.

Teddy grabbed her hand, "Are ye okay Gen?"

Genevieve had to close her eyes. "I will be," she whispered. A nurse assisting the doctor, reapplied fresh dressings and attended to the IV and catheter bag.

Before the doctor left he said, "Mrs. Walker, let me know if you need me for anything. You're doing very well. The wounds are healing with no signs of infection. Try and get some rest soon."

Genevieve took the doctor's hand, "Thank you. Thank you for saving my life."

The doctor squeezed her hand, "I admire your outlook on adversity Mrs. Walker. Most people can't see a rainbow in all of this. But it is *that* attitude which will heal those wounds, much better than anything I could do."

As the doctor exited the room, Genevieve contemplated his final words. *A rainbow attitude. I suppose it could be interpreted that way.* Genevieve was good at lifting others up, which was what her talk with Broc was all about. It was imperative that he not feel blame. But inside, the hurt was more than the physical wounds. After all, Genevieve was only human. Why did this have to happen to her? Did she draw this pain upon herself?

For the first time, she thought of the person in the other car. *What happened to them?*

CHAPTER 37

THE END OF ONE PAIN

JUST THEN, THE hospital door opened, and Uncle Steven and Aunt Melinda came in. Genevieve's brave facade quickly dissolved into tears at the sight of her cherished guardians. As they moved closer, Genevieve regressed to the child she once was…lost and sad. Reaching out her arms, all she wanted, all she *craved*, was her aunt and uncle's loving embrace.

And that, they gave her. Knowing that her children weren't nearby, Genevieve let her defenses down and cried uncontrollably. It was cathartic, releasing all the hurt. Aunt Melinda sat on the edge of the bed, holding Genevieve's hand and whispered, "It's all going to be okay, Honey."

Trying to gain some composure, Genevieve took a deep breath. As she let it out, she glanced over at Teddy who was wiping a tear away. *My sweet Love,* she thought. "I'm so sorry, Honey. I thought I could hold it together." Turning to her aunt and uncle, "Then I saw you." Genevieve's lip started to quiver, and tears filled her eye's again. "I'm so glad you are here. I have missed you so very much."

Aunt Melinda brushed tears from her eye's, as Uncle Steven turned away to hide his emotions. Aunt Melinda spoke softly, "You are *our* child, Genevieve. I may not have given birth to you, but my love runs as deep as your mothers ever did, and Uncle Steven is your dad in every sense of the word, you have to know that. As soon as Teddy called us, we were on a plane here. We've been staying at the house with Teddy and Broc, and we won't leave your side as long as you need us. Tess flew in last night. She sat with you for hours, but we told her to go and get some rest. She's at your house now, but will be back in a while."

Genevieve reached over and grabbed her uncle's hand. She could see the hurt in his face and felt the same remorse that mirrored her own. "I love you, so much! I had no right to say the things I did. The two of you have done nothing but love me, and for that I punished you. Every day I wish I could have taken my words back. Teddy urged me to call, many times, but I was so ashamed and the longer it went, the harder it was to swallow my pride and make things right again. I tell my children not to look back; to move forward without blame or regret, yet, I only have myself to blame, and regret haunts me every day. Aunt Melinda is exactly right. I couldn't have asked for better parents than the two of you. I've always known that."

Aunt Melinda looked at her husband, then back at Genevieve. "There were things about your mother we should have told you, yes. But, we were afraid of what it would do to you and your sister. You both were moving on, and we had hoped you would never know what she had done. Uncle Steven and I both underestimated your inner strength, Genevieve. You don't get to take all the blame and regret, for we have harbored so much of it ourselves."

Listening to Aunt Melinda gave Genevieve such relief. Now, reflecting on the unanswered questions of "why" the accident happened, Genevieve suddenly had a flash of insight, and a grin began to develop on her face. "It may sound crazy, but I just realized the purpose behind what happened to me. I see a 'rainbow' beyond all the rain or, Aunt Melinda, I now can actually see the 'good' in this. Aunt Melinda had a pleased look on her face as she and Genevieve locked eyes for a few moments. Genevieve smiled broadly, "The accident was a way back to you. And, although I want this physical pain to stop, I know it will--it's only temporary, compared to the endless suffering I had without the two of you in my life."

Genevieve pulled her aunt and uncle toward her. She could never have those precious five years back, but would do everything in her power to make things as they once were.

As Genevieve talked with her aunt and uncle, the joy and relief she felt, momentarily enveloped the physical pain which was astonishing. For a short time, Genevieve felt no pain, whatsoever, as she relished being with her aunt and uncle again.

When Ella and Broc came back into the room, everyone's mood was upbeat. Uncle Steven had new jokes to tell Broc and Teddy. As Genevieve strained to listen to them she thought, *Wow, they've become a lot more edgy than the ones he used to tell!* While the men sat huddled together in the corner of the room, Ella and Aunt Melinda tried to engage Genevieve in plans to do a river cruise along the Danube. But, between the strong drugs, emotions that had run the gamut, and her body screaming for rest, Genevieve could feel her eye's becoming heavier and heavier.

The last thing she remembered hearing as Aunt Melinda, sat, still holding Genevieve's hand was, "Sleep well my precious daughter." Soon voices became muffled and distant, and Genevieve drifted into peaceful silence.

CHAPTER 38

─── ❧ ❧ ───

WHEN "THE GOOD" IS ELUSIVE

WHEN GENEVIEVE OPENED her eyes, it was dark outside. No one was in the room. The only sound was the constant low beep of her heartbeat on the monitor. The dull throbbing in her head persisted. Reaching up, Genevieve felt the jagged stitches around the shaved spot on the back of her head. She adjusted her head slightly on the pillow to keep it from pressing on the wound. After she felt more comfortable, Genevieve's mind began to wander. *My car,* she thought. *And I just had a tune-up done!... What day is it? Who's been handling things at home, the things I normally do?* Genevieve looked at the clock on the side of the bed, *7:30 p.m. I feel hungry.* Genevieve reached down at her side and pushed the call button so a nurse could order her a tray of food. As she waited for a response, her mind drifted back to the accident. *I remember the light turning green. I remember turning... I remember seeing the car now. There wasn't one, but two people in it.*

Just then Tess walked in with Teddy.

"Tess," Genevieve softly cooed.

Tess ran to the bed and carefully gave her sister a long hug. "I'm sorry I wasn't here earlier, when you woke up. How are you feeling?"

Genevieve grabbed the button and pushed on it again, "Hungry! Everything hurts, but give it a week or so, and I'll be good as new."

Tess smiled and took Genevieve's hand. "I wish I had been around to see the big reunion. I'm so glad Gen."

Genevieve took a deep breath, "No one, and I mean *no one* is happier than I am. How are Ryan and the girls?"

Tess rolled her eyes. "Be glad you didn't have two preteen girls, Gen. It's double the trouble. But they're all doing fine. Ryan wanted to come, but someone had to stay behind with Selene and Sara."

Genevieve nodded, "Of course. I'm so glad you're here, Tess."

Looking up at Teddy, Genevieve could see some concern on his face. "Is everything okay Teddy?"

Tess looked at Teddy, then back at Genevieve. "I'll go see where that food is." Giving Genevieve a quick kiss on the cheek, "I'll be back in a little while."

As the door closed, Teddy walked over and sat in the chair next to the bed. "How *are* ye feeling, Love?"

Genevieve wanted to turn on her right side, so that she could see Teddy head on, but, since she couldn't, she positioned her bed so she could sit upright. "I'm doing okay. I think it's a good sign that I'm hungry, right?"

Teddy smiled. "That's a great sign Gen. But if the hospital food makes ye lose your appetite, just let me know and I'll sneak in some of that greasy chicken ye love."

Genevieve put her thumb up, "Deal."

Teddy's smile began to fade again, and Genevieve knew something was up. "Okay, I know something is bothering you. What aren't you telling me?"

Teddy got up from the chair. "Gen, I need to talk to ye about the accident, about the people in the other car."

Genevieve replied, "I've been wondering about that for a while now. Just before you and Tess came in, I remembered seeing two people in the car just before it hit me. What happened to them? Are they going to be alright?"

Teddy looked at his wife, "Ye saw the people in the car?"

Genevieve nodded. "It's a blur, but I can remember there were two people...why?" Teddy sat back down, slumping in the chair. The reaction he was displaying alarmed Genevieve. "What Teddy, tell me!" She grabbed his arm and quickly felt acute despair and powerlessness.

"Gen, ye knew someone in that car. It was Cindy, Sol's wife."

Genevieve shook her head frowning. She closed her eyes, trying to focus on the images in her mind as the car rushed toward her. *That can't be right. I would have seen her.* Pressing her memory, a snapshot of a man behind the wheel was all that appeared. "I remember a man. A man was driving. There wasn't any time to see the other person. You said it was Cindy? Who was with her? I know it wasn't Sol. Is she okay?"

Teddy slowly shook his head. "No Gen. I've been looking for the right time to tell ye. Cindy died in the accident."

Gasping, Genevieve shook her head. Everything suddenly became surreal again. Genevieve felt lightheaded, her appetite vanished. *Cindy!* As realization started to set in, Genevieve began to moan, her pain suddenly became more acute. "I don't understand."

Getting up again, Teddy walked over to the window and looked out into the dark parking lot. "I guess it's best that I start from the beginning. Something I nivvor told ye about Sol and Cindy." Genevieve could feel her heart pounding as she waited for Teddy to continue. "A couple of months ago, Sol found oot that Cindy was having an affair. It had been going on for a while. They separated right affta. That was the man she was with in the car. His name is Greg. He received some serious injuries in the crash, but he'll eventually be okay."

Genevieve's head was spinning. Wiping her wet eyes, "You're telling me, that *Cindy* was the one that was unfaithful? It doesn't make any sense. It was obvious, how much she adored Sol."

Teddy interjected, "I know, she did. But, I guess there was a lot of mistrust on her part, thought Sol had women on the side...it's a long story. Sol said he'd been trying to get her back. This has hit him very hard. I tried calling him just before I came but he won't answer the phone, so I called his son to go and check on him.

"On the day of the accident, I wondered why ye hadn't come back home after dropping Broc off at practice, but thought maybe ye had gone shopping. It was aboot the time ye were to pick Broc up that I got a call from the hospital. They said my wife had been in an accident and it didn't look like she'd make it, to get there as soon as I could. By then Sol had got word about Cindy as well. We both thought we had lost our wives that day. Your life was touch and go for the first twenty-four hours, Gen.

"I just couldn't understand what happened. I needed to know why. Yesterday, I went to Greg's hospital room, to talk to him. A lass was leaving his room just as I got there, so I spoke to her instead. I found oot it was his daughter, Sheena. I told her my wife was the woman in the other car. I said I just wanted to know why her fatha ran the red light and was driving so fast. The poor girl broke down, said she was so sorry for what happened to ye. She told me her fatha and his girlfriend, Cindy, were arguing. That Cindy wanted to leave him and go back to her husband. Sheena said she nivvor knew her father's girlfriend was even married. She went on to say that Cindy demanded that her fatha, pull over, but instead, he sped up as they continued to yell at each other.

"I told Sol all this last night. I thought he'd want to know how Cindy felt…that she still loved him and had wanted to come back to him. I didn't want him to feel betrayed to the end. "Now, I wonder if it was the right thing to do. Was it Gen?"

Genevieve had kept her distance from Sol for several years, after a simple, innocent embrace, revealed lustful feelings he had that were totally inappropriate toward her. She could understand why Cindy would have felt insecure, as Sol was quite the social peacock, unfurling his feathers at parties, and strutting around. But in the end, Genevieve didn't think Sol would ever pursue his impulses. She knew he loved his wife and probably thought they were on solid footing until the day she left.

"If it were me, I'd want to know. Sol will never have her back, but to know that she still loved him and wanted to go back to him should give him some comfort."

Teddy looked relieved. As Genevieve took his hand in hers, she began to grasp how much he had been dealing with. The myriad of critical concerns that sat squarely on his shoulders. Genevieve could feel the heaviness of each emotion and saw the exhaustion talking its toll.

"When was the last time you got some real rest, Teddy?"

Rubbing his eyes with his free hand, he started to yawn. "I catch a little here and there."

Genevieve released his hand and used her fingers to comb through his hair. "I'm fine now, really I am. When Tess comes back, I'd like to visit just a little bit longer, and then I want the both of you to go home and get a good night's rest. God, I love you Teddy. I'm so sorry for all you have had to deal with. Not only with me but with Sol too."

151

Teddy grabbed Genevieve's hand and held it tight. "I can deal with anything as long as I have ye. I just don't know what I'd do if I lost ye, Gen." Kissing her hand, he acknowledged, "I think I will sleep like a rock tonight."

There was a knock at the door, and then Tess peeked in. "I scrounged up some food for you, Sis. It will do for tonight, but I think it's been sitting around longer than it should."

Genevieve lifted the cover and placed it back down. "Thanks. I'll give it a try in a little bit. Where have you been?"

Tess' demeanor changed, and she looked disturbed. "Well, I went downstairs to the cafeteria, when I saw several security guards run outside. I bought a sandwich for myself and sat down to eat it before getting you that wonderful dinner sitting there, before you. About fifteen minutes later, a different security officer came in and started to talk to the woman behind the counter. I guess some guy was in the parking lot and shot and killed himself."

Teddy and Genevieve looked at each other for several moments before Teddy spoke, "Did ye hear anything else?"

Tess shook her head, "Not really, just that it made a mess of his cherry red jeep."

CHAPTER 39

PARTING WORDS

To Ted

Hey Buddy. I want to thank you for being a good partner and even better friend. I'm so glad Genevieve will be okay.

I haven't been honest with you about some personal things. Things I can't even tell you now, although you probably will find out sooner or later.

I came here, to the hospital, to kill Greg. I hate the man for all he's taken from me. But, upon reflection, as I sit here with the gun in my lap, I realize he is all his daughter, Sheena has now, and I can't take that away from her.

Instead, I'll go to be with my Cindy. She must be so lost and scared.

I wish you all the happiness you deserve Ted, including a business partner that fits your ideals better than I ever did...your daughter comes to mind.

Whatever you do, don't mourn for me. Be at peace Ted, I am.

Sol

PART SIX

CHOICES AT 59 YEARS OLD

BACK AT THE PARTY...

ROSA WATCHED A tear move down Genevieve's face as she continued to sleep.

"She's crying," observed Kalinda, who had been at Genevieve's dinner table, and now stood at the edge of the couch along with everyone else from the party.

Rosa nodded. "Yes, I see that. Her emotions have been near the surface the entire time she has fallen into this unconscious state."

Kalinda continued to inquire, "How long do you think this will go on?"

Rosa stared at Genevieve and wiped the tear from her face. Tilting her head to the side, Rosa lamented, "I feel that when the dream ends, so will our time with her."

Genevieve wanted to wake up. She'd had enough after the last torturous discovery. But was she really asleep, or was she somewhere beyond slumber? Like a dream that flees beyond your reach to recollect, Genevieve felt her question racing away into oblivion as she sensed a new reality opening up around her.

Feeling the warmth of the sun and laughter all around, Genevieve took a deep breath and dove into age fifty-nine.

CHAPTER 40

─── ⚬₵₰₂₰ ───

AGE 59
CHOICE ONE

WHEW! NOW THAT feels good! Genevieve could feel her heated skin quickly cool down as she trolled under the water, ready to grab her unsuspecting grandson. Pulling his legs from under him, she popped up as he screamed with surprise. "Grandma! Not fair, I didn't see you coming."

As Genevieve bent down in the shallow pool water to be eye to eye with Steve, Ella's ten-year-old middle child, she whispered in his wet ear, "That's the whole point, Mister!" As she tried to run away in the resistant water, the rest of the Three Musketeers made their attack. Steve jumped from behind as his brother's Rich, twelve-years-old, and Zeff, nine, pulled at her arms, knocking her under the water. Racing to get to safety, Genevieve barely made it to the top steps before Rich took a final lunge at her leg but missed.

Genevieve loved her time with her grandchildren. It was so different now, not having that "motherly" responsibility for these children like she had when raising Ella and Broc. The task of raising a happy, well-balanced child can be overwhelming at times, never knowing if all you have to give will ever be enough. It was a refreshing freedom to just take these moments and relish them without other concerns.

As she sat down next to Ella, Genevieve knew how smart and competent her daughter was, and could always feel her intense love for her children as well as the ebb and flow of insecure feelings Genevieve had known herself... that all caring mothers have.

It was natural, Genevieve considered. *A small dose of doubt isn't necessarily a bad thing, because it makes you aware you have the wrong perspective about who you are and what you can do.* The unwanted feeling, Genevieve had come to believe, was your true Self, or Soul, letting you know you were misguided. If you were to persist in the negative thinking about yourself, it would do what it could to change that perspective. Most of the time, you would be unaware of what was being done on your behalf, as people, places, memories and events would be sent to you in the form of inspiration and guidance. Soon, your perspective would be altered and you would *know* who you were again and what you always knew you could do. Confidence would surge as well as your emotions.

But heed the warning, pay attention to the feeling, as it can be insidious if left to feed unfettered. Genevieve knew only too well, how doubt could bring a person to their knees, or worse.

Genevieve and Ella sat watching as the boys burned energy in the pool when Ella inquired, "So, you leave tomorrow for Arizona then?"

Genevieve stared blankly ahead, "I guess I better, I've held everything up long enough. It's time to finalize everything. It's just been so hard to go back, now that Aunt Melinda and Uncle Steven are gone. I wish your father were with me right now." Ella reminded her mother that she would take the trip with her as Finn, Ella's husband, was quite capable of handling their brood himself, but Genevieve assured her daughter she'd be fine.

Ella continued to her next question, "When do you plan to go to England and join Dad?"

Genevieve turned to look at Ella with a reassuring smile, "Soon, Honey, soon. I miss that man so much, but I really need to finalize things now. It's not fair to Tess or the staff at the estate to continue in a state of limbo. It's probably better anyway that I take the trip by myself. It's so emotional for me, and your dad feels so bad when he can't find any way to console me. It was hard to see him go after the funeral, but I had to force him onto the plane. You know your father, he never thinks of himself first. But he had already delayed the trip for weeks, and he had been *so* looking forward to spending time there...so had I."

As Genevieve and Ella continued to talk, a half hour quickly passed. Not realizing the lateness of the hour, Ella quickly called for the boys to get out of the pool. "I better get home and see if Finn has started any dinner. Otherwise, it's going to be pizza night."

Genevieve waved as Ella's van left the driveway, then closed the door. *I better get some bags packed I guess. I hope I can fly straight from Arizona to London in a few days from now. The sooner the better.* With a glance at the clock, *Rats, it's getting late in Florida. I wish Tess lived closer to us. I better give her a call now and make sure our arrival times are still close together.*

Leaving the living room, Genevieve stopped for a moment to look at a wedding picture of Broc and his wife, Adira. *Such a handsome couple. I wondered when my boy would find the right one for him. He never got seriously attached to anyone in high school. I guess he was like me, knowing the right person was out there, just like I did when I met his father. Now he's going to be a father in a few months, and I'll be a grandma again...to a girl! I can't wait to see her.* While Broc and Adira only lived a few hours away, it was too far for Genevieve's liking.

Broc found his calling in college when he went with a friend to hear a speaker talking about endangered marine life. It triggered something within him, and he became obsessed with all life beneath the sea. At the end of the semester, he changed his General Education major to Marine Biology. Since there was a wait to get into the college he wanted, he spent a semester taking local biology classes and took a job at a pet store, where he began to learn about the care of fish and their fragile environment. Finally, he moved a semester later to San Francisco and attended San Francisco State University. It was also where he met Adira, while attending one of his many biology classes. Now living in Monterey, Broc works as one of the research scientists at the Monterey Bay Aquarium and Adira teaches 4th grade at a private school in Marina, a town nearby. *I sure hope I'm back home before the baby is born.* Genevieve sighed.

Going up the stairs, Genevieve heard the phone ring and ran to her bedroom to answer it. "Hello?"

Sounding as if he was in the next room, "Is that my bride speaking?"

Genevieve smiled, "I was hoping it might be you, but it's the middle of the night there, why aren't you sleeping?"

Teddy explained, "I won't be around when ye leave tomorrow, so a little missed sleep is worth hearing your voice. I really miss ye."

It took very little to get Genevieve crying these days, and her eyes became blurred by tears, not yet fallen. All that she could muster was a whispered, "I miss you too."

Teddy paused and must have sensed Genevieve's mood. "It's almost done, Gen. Before ye know it, we'll be sitting on the beach drinking some fine ale. In fact, I've been test tasting quite a few!"

Genevieve wiped her eyes and smiled. "Oh, you have, have you. Well, you better find me a good pale, as you know, I can't quite stomach that dark stuff."

Teddy laughed, "Aye, I know you're a lightweight. Do ye think ye can be coming this way soon?"

Genevieve shrugged. "I sure hope so. I really just want to get the most urgent issues finalized. Maybe Tess and Ryan can stay on longer and help the staff in cataloging everything. Otherwise, I may just wait to do that after we come back from England, so you can be with me."

Teddy quipped, "That works for me. Just get over here as soon as ye can. The next two days I will be doing some traveling around, so let's talk day affta tomorrow. By then ye should have a betta idea on what needs to be done and when ye can be on your way here. Amelie is really anxious to see ye, Gen."

Genevieve smiled, "That sister-in-law of mine is trouble! I can't wait to see what mischief she's been up to!"

After they had said their good-byes, Genevieve turned on the T.V. for company and got to work with packing, but her eyes kept diverting to a framed snapshot on the nightstand of her and Teddy in their early twenties, wrapped in a tight embrace, kissing. *He still takes my breath away.*

CHAPTER 41

COMING HOME

As Genevieve maneuvered her way to her seat, 18F, a man already was sitting in 18D. *Men and their aisle seats.* Teddy was an aisle man too, as was Uncle Steven, and, even though growing up Genevieve flew mostly first class where there was much more room, these days unless it was a really long flight, coach was fine.

After the gentleman had stood up, Genevieve crawled over to her seat, accidently pulling the lady's hair in the seat in front of her as Genevieve grabbed at the seat for balance. "Sorry! I'm sorry," Genevieve said in a loud whisper, as the woman gave her an annoyed glance. *Great start Genevieve.*

Luckily, the rest of the flight went smoothly, other than hitting her head on the overhead bin on her way out.

Genevieve watched a large clock on the wall as she waited for her suitcases. 1:10 p.m. *I was supposed to meet Tess and Ryan out front at 1:00 p.m. Hurry up luggage!* Finally, her bags appeared, and with the help of a man standing next to her, she hoisted the oversized bags onto a carrier and hurried toward the exit.

Spotting Tess and Ryan as soon as she was out the door, Ryan ran to help with the luggage. "Good timing Gen, we arrived an hour ago and just picked up the rental car."

Genevieve let out a sigh of relief. "Oh my gosh, good to hear! Ryan, I want to thank you and Tess for being so patient with me." Ryan dismissed the concern and gave Genevieve a kiss on the cheek.

At the car, Tess hurried over and pulled Genevieve close with a tight hug. "Ah, Genevieve, I wish I could help you through this. I know it's been especially hard on you."

As Genevieve helped Ryan lift her heaviest bag into the trunk, she replied, "It was just so sudden, no time to prepare. After years estranged, we were back to the way we used to be. Things were *so* good Tess. I had a great visit with them just a few months ago. Then, just before Teddy and I are supposed to leave for England, I get a call saying they were dead, killed in a car crash.

"I guess what hurts, even more, is the fact that they were on their way to visit us, after a few weeks to see some California sites. I was really looking forward to seeing them after I got back from England, hoping they would stay until Broc's new baby was born. But I could see that Uncle Steven's reaction time was slowing way down. I should have insisted they fly, but he said he was doing just fine, that he'd take it slow."

While driving to the estate, the conversation changed to the latest happenings of each of their families. Tess' daughter, Selene, still not married, or interested in anyone as far as Tess and Ryan knew, worked for a South American tour company, contracting with sightseeing vendors, transportation companies, and hotels, then packaging them together. But whenever she got the chance, Selene helped in guiding a tour or two which is what she really loved the most. They didn't talk that much about their daughter Sara, other than what Genevieve was already well aware. She was married, had two small girls and worked full-time as a hair stylist. Genevieve sensed there was something Tess wasn't telling her, but she didn't pry.

Before she knew it, they were at the large gate leading to the estate. Once opened, they drove through the immaculate grounds, something Uncle Steven was a stickler about maintaining. He would go through one gardening crew after another until he found the one that met his expectations. But with everyone her aunt and uncle employed, good work was well compensated.

Parking the car at the front entrance, Gidda, Aunt Melinda's head housekeeper, and now the only one still maintaining the ten bedroom, ten bath home, ran out to greet them. Genevieve always braced herself when Gidda was about to give one of her hugs--Gidda wasn't known for her gentle touch.

What she was known for was her compassion and loyalty. There were rumors that Gidda had several job offers but she was refusing to consider any of them, even if it meant losing an excellent employment package, until she was no longer needed at the estate. That was one of the reasons Genevieve needed to move forward...so everyone else could, as well.

After all the luggage had been put away, the three settled in the living room, the gathering place. Every time Genevieve came home, Aunt Melinda had added another picture or two to the overwhelming gallery. As she roamed around the room, indeed more had been added since the last time she visited.

The most prominent was the portrait that was done when the girls were young. Staring at it, Genevieve remembered how boring and uncomfortable it was to sit while the painter worked at his art. Tess, although five at the time, acted more like three, wiggling and crying, but then again, *she* just got away with something Genevieve wished she could have done as well.

It was all worth it though. The painter was magical in how he brought out the little nuances in each of them. From Uncle Steven's funny cowlick along his hairline, and his infectious laughing eyes, to the small scar Genevieve had on her hand when she cut it falling off a horse when she was twelve. Aunt Melinda wore her signature red lipstick and one of her beautiful royal blue knit dresses that showed off her perfect figure--perfectly. The painter captured the pride Aunt Melinda had for her family in the tilt of her head and the way he made her eyes twinkle. He even captured a bit of Tess' demeanor that day, for although she had a big smile displaying two missing front teeth, you could see a hint of a frown in the scrunching of her eyebrows.

As Tess, Ryan and Genevieve laughed and reminisced, Gidda popped her head in to say dinner would be ready in about two hours. While the other two chose to go get showered, and rest a bit before dinner, Genevieve decided to take a walk to the old stable.

CHAPTER 42

WHAT LIES BENEATH THE EARTH?

WALKING PAST THE large pool, Genevieve couldn't resist and, after taking her sandals off, submerged her feet on the first step. The pool felt almost like bathwater. No wonder, since Gidda had said the Arizona sun had been particularly punishing that last week with daytime temperatures holding around 110 degrees. Slipping her shoes back on, she hurried past the vast open grounds until she reached the stable.

It was so quiet. Long ago, there was barely enough room for all their horses, now, only one sweet filly named Piper graced the hallowed stable grounds. Genevieve could still remember the satisfaction on Uncle Steven's face when showing off his panoply of show horses to friends and colleagues.

The closer Genevieve got to Piper, who took residence in the very first stall, the more excited the young filly got, snorting and prancing for her attention. "Hi there, little girl."

Genevieve looked down the dark aisle, pausing at the stall which Haddie, her horse, had called home for many years. After rubbing the bridge of Piper's nose for a few minutes and having a one-sided conversation, Genevieve decided to stroll the place that gave her such comfort, particularly in her early days when she was a new resident herself.

Back and forth she slowly paced, envisioning the way it had been in its heyday, with the groomers and trainers moving the horses in and out. The pungent smell of fresh hay being disbursed in the stalls. The unique sounds of a menagerie of breeds, yet, all speaking the language of *Equus caballus*. Genevieve was in awe of the animals as a child, soaking up everything she could to understand and communicate with them better.

As Genevieve passed Haddie's stall for the third time, she stopped and opened the gate. No remnant signs of her ever being there remained. Shutting the gate behind her, Genevieve closed her eyes, imagining the feeling of Haddie's hot, moist breath on her neck when she used to nudge Genevieve for attention. *You can't go back Haddie, can you?* As Genevieve started to leave the stall, she heard a strange noise below her foot. With a puzzled look, Genevieve pressed the spot again. It made a creaking sound. *What in the world?* Kneeling down, Genevieve brushed the dry hay to expose a small metal covering, small hinges on one side and a padlock on the other.

Where did this come from, and when? It certainly was never here when I lived here. As she rattled the lock, it sounded hollow beneath the metal plate. Sitting back and staring at it as if it had just fallen from the sky, Genevieve couldn't make sense of the discovery. *Why would this be here?* Looking around at the desolate surroundings in which the area had become, she deduced, *It's a perfect place to hide something. The stable was all but empty now, and only Uncle Steven or Jeremy, the groom, would have any reason to venture out here since Aunt Melinda stopped coming out here a long time ago when arthritis in her hips made it too difficult to ride.*

Looking at her watch, Genevieve had to hurry back and get cleaned up for dinner. Brushing the hay back over the metal, Genevieve got up and quickly said a hasty good-bye to Piper with a promise to be back soon with a snack.

When dinner was served, the trio coaxed Gidda to eat with them. She brought them up to date on the happenings at the estate and which of the workers had been looking for new employment. Genevieve tried to stay focused on the conversation at hand, but several times Tess had to repeat a question before Genevieve actually heard it. "Are you okay, Gen?" Tess frowned.

Genevieve gave a sleepy smile, "I'm just more exhausted than I thought. With a long day ahead of us tomorrow, I think I'll make it an early night if that's okay."

Tess nodded. "I think that sounds like a good idea. I'm still on Florida time anyway, so it certainly feels late to me."

After the dishes were done and everyone had called it a night, Genevieve headed back to the stable after finding the tools she would need and a few carrots for Piper.

The moon was almost full, giving off a radiant iridescence to everything below which was very helpful in guiding the way back. Piper had been asleep, and when Genevieve approached with a flashlight, it startled her. She made a loud whinny and stumbled jumping backward. "I'm sorry Piper, come back... it's okay." Genevieve drew her near as she dangled a carrot over the railing. When Piper had calmed down and finished the third carrot, looking for more, Genevieve put up her hands, "That's all I've got for now. Time to go back to sleep. It's past your bedtime." Picking up the crowbar she brought along, she used the flashlight to find Haddie's stall. Once inside, she targeted the spot and knelt down. Clearing the hay again, she pried at the latch, and without much effort it came off.

Secrets are secrets for a reason, Genevieve. What will I find down there? Genevieve slowly lifted the metal plate. Below was what looked like a tool box, wrapped in plastic. *I could just walk away now. It's not too late.* After a hesitant pause, she lifted the box which was surprisingly light. After unwrapping the plastic, she opened the box. Inside was a large notebook and below were pictures and other assorted papers.

Genevieve closed the box and moved herself and the box to the side of the stall. Leaning up against the sideboards, she opened the box again and stared at the worn, brown leather cover. Lifting the notebook, she placed it in her lap. She could still smell the richness of the leather as it had been curing in the hot earth for who knows how long. Genevieve's heart pounded heavily, as she opened the book. Glancing down she recognized her uncle's writing and read:

Not one that feels compelled to write my feelings, yet I have no one I can talk to...

With that, Genevieve closed the book quickly. She could see now that it was some type of journal or diary. Genevieve was well aware of the consequences of invading someone's personal feelings. This was no different. Emotions written in ink. Private feelings, hidden away.

Peering into the box, she noticed pictures of her aunt, glamorous pictures. As Genevieve started to rummage through the pile, she realized Aunt

Melinda had to have been a model. *Why didn't she ever tell me? I always thought she dressed, even acted like one, the way she carried herself. God, she was beautiful!* Then another picture caught her eye. This one was of her aunt and uncle. It was a candid picture but definitely taken by a photographer, as it had the same shiny finish her modeling pictures had. The photographer captured a close-up of the two of them in a passionate kiss. *Why would he hide such an amazing picture away like this?*

There were no other pictures in the box of anyone that Genevieve recognized. But as she flipped from picture to picture, she didn't need to read his journal to understand why he placed it far out where Aunt Melinda would never find it.

THE CHILD NEVER SPOKEN OF

THE ONLY PICTURES left in the box were of a little girl, as young as two months, and spanning all the way to adulthood. On the back of each one, in the same penmanship, the words "Faye" the year and her age. Examining the year on the back of her first picture at 2 ½ months old, Genevieve realized Faye was the same age she was. *Not only was she born the same year as me, but it was also the same year Aunt Melinda and Uncle Steven were married.* Besides the handful of photos, there were scattered report cards and a few miscellaneous documents.

She never knew you had a child. That's why you hid it out here, where she'd never find it.

It didn't matter to Genevieve how or when Faye had come into the world. If it had been before Uncle Steven married Aunt Melinda, there had to be a reason he never told her. If it had been the result of an affair, Genevieve refused to judge. She had done enough of that to last a lifetime...and now their lifetime was over, water under the bridge.

All Genevieve knew and had no doubt of, was that her aunt and uncle had a wonderful life together. She never once doubted their love for each other. It was always evident in the way they behaved together. Genevieve, while growing up, often caught the two of them in, what could only be described as an intense "loving stare" eyes locked on each other as if nothing else existed. It was *their* example that showed Genevieve how a true, loving relationship looked and acted.

The fact that Uncle Steven kept everything and hid it in the stable, meant he cared about Faye, otherwise why go to such great pains to hold onto these memories? Who sent him the photos, Faye's mother? He must have asked her to send them, after all, Faye was a part of him. As Genevieve studied a picture of Faye at seventeen, she thought she looked familiar, but couldn't figure out why. Still, she didn't seem to have any noticeable traits that matched Uncle Steven, deducing Faye must resemble her mother. *All those times you seemed to have that faraway look Uncle, were you thinking about her? From time to time, did you come out here to the stable, and look at these pictures with regret, knowing Aunt Melinda could never carry a child for you?*

Did Tess and I fill that void for you? God, I hope we did.

As Genevieve started to put all the pictures back in the tool box, she noticed a faded newspaper clipping. It was an obituary...for Faye. It said she died in a car accident at the age of forty-one. All of a sudden Genevieve felt terrible anguish tightening in her chest. *She died while you and I were estranged.* Soon Genevieve's guilt swept over her, imagining how he must have felt, and she dissolved into tears. *You already felt you had lost me, then you get this news. Where were you on that day? Was there anyone to talk to, to console you?*

Looking at the notebook, Genevieve assumed many of the questions might be answered there. But what if it only added more? *Does any of it really matter now anyway? Everyone is gone. You're gone, Aunt Melinda is gone and Faye--she's gone too. Delving into your personal diary may cause more heartache than I could bear, and you mean too much to me to risk that.*

Genevieve looked at each picture one more time as she placed it in the box. When she got to the picture of her aunt and uncle and those of her aunt modeling, she laid them aside. Finally placing the notebook back in the box, Genevieve closed the latch. *What would be the purpose of putting everything back in the ground where I found it? Would the next person to discover it exploit history to make a buck? Or extort us to keep your legacy all that it is and forever should be?*

Genevieve didn't know if it was supposed to be her destiny to find it. There was nothing she could do with the knowledge now that Faye was gone, and for what other purpose would Uncle Steven want it to be found? He had so much to lose otherwise. Still, a nagging question remained. *Why of all places, did you hide it in Haddie's stall?*

It's a question that can never be answered. I have to let it go, and it's time you let go too, Uncle. I'll hold your secret close to my heart. I know Faye was in that eternal place, waiting to wrap her arms around you and welcome you home, with no guilt, no judgment, just as I will make sure it remains here, on earth.

Getting up, Genevieve walked to the back of the stable where she knew some old barrels sat. Finding some matches in the tool shed nearby, she put all contents of the tool box in the barrel and burned them.

When only embers were left glowing, Genevieve took a hose and doused the ashes. Gathering the pictures she had put aside, she made her way back to the house and went to bed.

CHAPTER 44

PICTURES DON'T TELL THE TALE

HEARING MUFFLED NOISES, Genevieve pried her eyes open and looked at the clock. 6:35 A.M. *I guess I'd be rearing to go too if I had gone to bed when I said I was going to!* Next to the clock were the pictures she had saved from the night before. *I couldn't get rid of these. I still don't know why Aunt Melinda never talked of those days. By all account, she looked very successful as a model. And this picture of the two of them, it's how I always want to remember them.*

Going to the suitcase, Genevieve pulled out some shorts and the coolest sleeveless shirt she could find. The sun was already warning her, from the glare coming through the window, that it wasn't ready to cool things down yet. Before going downstairs to breakfast, Genevieve decided she better pull a dress out of the suitcase to change into later in the day. Going to the closet to hang it up, she found that Aunt Melinda had already filled it to overflowing with her own clothes. The rather large, walk-in closet that once was Genevieve's was now filled with memories of her aunt. *This is going to take a while to go through. I can see that now.*

After squeezing her summer dress in between the tightly packed wardrobe of her aunt's, Genevieve ran her fingers along the beautifully tailored clothes. So many of them Genevieve could still picture her aunt wearing. Then Genevieve gasped, *It's that gown, the one she wore in the picture.* Aunt Melinda had worn the elegant red gown on a fashion show runway. In the picture, her hair was dark, pulled tight in a slick bun behind her head. She wore elegant long earrings, dripping with rubies and a diamond studded bangle bracelet, yet her neck was bare. The make-up was dramatic, with dark mascara and she wore the exact same lip color as the color of her deep red gown.

172

The designer's vision was all about shimmering elegance. With a slit, high on the thigh, there was no one better equipped than Aunt Melinda, whose long shapely legs enhanced that aspect of the dress better than any other model ever could. It was a form-fitting masterpiece. It glittered and sparkled, sleeveless on one arm, full sleeve on the other. As Genevieve took the dress, that was wrapped in plastic and laid it on the bed, she could see how each tiny sequin had been sewn by hand. It had to have taken weeks or even longer to accomplish, with each row sewn to perfection. Genevieve grabbed the picture and compared it to the gown lying before her. *Identical.*

I always thought I knew everything there was to know about you and Uncle Steven. Is there more I'll find, tucked away behind an old book or taped to the back of a picture frame? Was the world Tess and I lived in an illusion?

Maybe life is anyway, she pondered. *We see what we choose to see, believe what we are told, so our world can make sense to us; so we can fit in and feel normal. I still, and always will, believe we were a happy family. That whatever happened, hidden away in your and Uncle Steven's past, never affected what we all had together as a family. If in the end, it was just an illusion, then I gladly choose the fantasy I lived.*

Placing the gown back in the closet, Genevieve grabbed the pictures and headed downstairs. *Wait 'til Tess feasts her eyes on these!*

The alluring smell of breakfast drew Genevieve down the stairs in a hurry. Aunt Melinda and Uncle Steven always bought all their beef, pork and poultry from local ranchers and stored it in a large freezer in the gigantic kitchen pantry. There was something about the way the bacon was cured; the way it had its own unique taste and smell that drove Genevieve crazy.

When she walked into the kitchen, Tess and Ryan were almost done eating. Genevieve walked over and gave each a quick hug before sitting down next to them, placing the pictures next to her. "BACON!" Genevieve shouted, making Gidda jump as she cleaned dishes in the sink.

Turning and putting her hand over her heart, Gidda let out a heavy breath and smiled, "I made plenty, but I see it may not be enough now," giving Ryan a little frown. "I'll cook a little more."

Genevieve jumped in, "No Gidda, six slices is more than enough, thank you."

Gidda returned with a smile and shrugged, "Okay then. I'll bring you some coffee, just cream, yes?" Genevieve nodded.

Tess noticed the pictures next to her sister. "What do you have there, Gen?"

Before Genevieve grabbed a slice of greasy bacon, she lifted the pictures and laid them next to Tess. "I found these last night as I was rummaging around in my bedroom."

Tess picked them up carefully. "Oh my God, she was a model?"

Genevieve nodded. "It sure looks like it, and an incredible one too. No wonder she always looked so poised and loved fashion so much."

Tess kept staring at the five different photos of her aunt in various outfits and poses. "Why didn't she ever tell us? Why did she quit?"

Genevieve shook her head. "I don't know. I keep asking the same question. Mom never mentioned it either when I was young. It should have been something the whole family was proud of." Genevieve pointed to the picture of her aunt in the red gown. "I found this dress in my closet. Tess, you wouldn't believe the incredible detail!"

Tess just kept staring in awe and disbelief for a couple more minutes, then pulled the picture of her aunt and uncle kissing from beneath the pile. Tears filled her eyes, then Genevieve's as well. In a whisper, Genevieve said, "This is how I'll remember them." Tess looked at her sister, wiping her face and nodded.

Tess and Ryan sat with Genevieve while she ate breakfast, making a plan for what they needed to try to accomplish that day. "Teddy is calling this afternoon, so I want to give him an idea as to when I can head on to England."

Tess pushed away from the table, "Then let's get down to work!"

The first thing Genevieve did was take the picture of her aunt and uncle and exchange it for one of hers in the living room. "It will give us inspiration," Genevieve said to Tess who had been watching.

The morning went quickly. There were things in the trust that were specified to be given to certain people, and Genevieve set about getting the items tagged and set aside from everything else. Her aunt and uncle's lawyer was stopping by soon as Genevieve wanted to go over the ten full-time employees' compensation packet. Only Gidda and two grounds men would remain until the estate was sold. Genevieve called an old-time friend of Uncle Steven's and asked if he would take Piper to his ranch. "I think he'd want you to have her, Redmond." He said he'd be honored to have the little filly to remind him of his dear friend.

Just before 1:00 p.m., the doorbell rang. Peering through the etched glass of the front doors, Genevieve could see it was Brennan Stoddard, her aunt and uncle's lawyer. Brennan was a well-known attorney in the Phoenix/Scottsdale area. In his late seventies now, and a widower, he had been their attorney for as long as Genevieve could remember. After the reading of the will last month, he lamented that he'd be retiring soon, hoping to have a little fun with the few friends he still had left.

Genevieve opened the door and gave Brennan a long hug. She could feel that he still felt the sting from the loss of his friend. "Come in Mr. Stoddard and thank you for making the trip."

As Brennan entered the open foyer, he stopped and looked around. "I suppose this will be the last time I visit this beautiful place." Genevieve's lips turned down slightly, realizing he probably was right.

Grabbing his arm, she led him to the living room which was empty for the moment. As they sat on the couch, Brennan pulled out the paperwork for Genevieve to sign. It was a very generous package for the staff, which included a year's salary, and their healthcare would be covered for the year as well. Besides that, Genevieve let them each take one thing, anything, as a remembrance, as long as it wasn't already designated for someone else.

When Brennan was putting the papers back in his briefcase, Genevieve walked over and grabbed the picture of her aunt and uncle and the modeling pictures lying next to it. "I want to show you something."

As she handed the pictures to Brennan, she could see him remembering something. He tipped his head to the side and smiled, only uttering, "Great pictures."

Genevieve blurted out, "I know about the girl, Faye."

175

Brennan looked at her in surprise. "How?"

Genevieve didn't want to go into the specifics, "I found things my uncle had saved in a box last night."

Brennan kept his stare on her and slowly nodded. "I see. It must have come as a big shock to you." Genevieve nodded.

Returning his gaze to the pictures, Brennan spoke softly, "I didn't know them then, but your uncle took me into his confidence. It was such a tragic event, horrific really. They were both so courageous."

Genevieve frowned. "Wait, my aunt knew about Faye?"

Brennan stopped short, realizing Genevieve didn't know the whole story after all. In a dismissive tone he said, "Oh, hey, I don't quite remember all the facts. I'm getting old, and it's all ancient history now anyway."

As Brennan got up and moved quickly to the door, he impressed upon Genevieve, "All that's important was how much they loved you and Tess. You two were their world. You kept them grounded and gave them the purpose they needed, never forget that. It is the one fact I *am* sure of." Looking at his watch he said, "I have an appointment coming up in an hour, so I better get going. I'll have the papers ready next week. I hear you're headed for England, be sure to give Ted my regards."

Genevieve closed the door and leaned against it, looking down at the floor. *Horrific, Tragedy? **They** were so courageous? God, why did I burn the book? What actually happened?*

CHAPTER 45

SAME EVENT
A DIFFERENT CHOICE

QUIETLY DIVING INTO her pool Genevieve shuddered, *Whoa, the cool water sure feels good!* In stealth mode, she crept up on her ten-year-old grandson Steven, and pulled his legs from under him. As he screamed in surprise, his two brothers, Rich and Zeff came to his aid with an attack of their own.

"BOYS!" Ella hollered, "You'll hurt your grandmother!"

Genevieve couldn't stop laughing. "What, these namby-pambys? Not on your life!" With that, Genevieve scrambled for the steps, as she knew all too well, she was no match when the three of them were on the attack.

Making it to the stairs, before any of them got a good hold on her, Genevieve sat back down, next to her svelte, tanned daughter. Watching as the boys pounced on each other in the water, Genevieve questioned, "I thought you said Finn would be here by now?"

Ella shook her head, "He called a few minutes ago. He probably won't make it. His game went into extra innings, and he's beat, said he's going to head home."

Looking at her mom, Ella took a deep breath and exhaled. "So, tomorrow you head for Arizona then."

Genevieve kept her gaze toward her grandchildren. "I guess I better make the trip. I just haven't been ready to make things final. I'm not sure how I'll feel going back home, now that Aunt Melinda and Uncle Steven are gone. But I can only do so much long distance. Tess is going to meet me there so that we can wrap things up."

Ella, turned her gaze toward her children and asked, "When are you making the trip to be with Dad? I'm guessing he's been missing you terribly."

Genevieve nodded. "Not as much as I've missed him. The unforeseen circumstances obviously changed all our plans, but I couldn't let him stay behind when he'd been looking forward to the trip to England for months. He was such a blessing during the funeral and delayed the trip as it was, by over two weeks. But, I could tell he was yearning to go back home for a while, so I insisted he go. I hope to head straight over after my trip to Arizona.

"Anyway, he sounds happy, spending a lot of time with your Aunt Amelie and her family, as well as visiting your grandmother, even though she doesn't recognize him anymore. I must admit, I wish he were going with me tomorrow. I don't remember a time he wasn't with me when I needed him."

Ella, sitting poised and upright in the chair, touched her mom's arm, "Mom, I can go with you. I told you that Finn already said he could handle the boys alone for a few days."

Genevieve gave a wry smile. "It's not that I can't do this by myself, Honey, I just miss your dad, that's all."

Sliding back in the lounge chair, Ella smiled at her mother. "When I was younger I used to get embarrassed the way you and Dad acted around each other; both with that starry-eyed look. It was kind of sickening to be around you two as a teenager, yet, still kind of comforting, when so many of my friends only lived with one parent by then.

"I remember one time my friend, Terra, you remember her, right?"

Genevieve lifted her eyes to the sky, sifting through the multitude of "best friends" Ella went through growing up. "Yes, I always thought she looked a lot like you."

Ella nodded, then gave her mother a puzzled look. "Anyway, one day, when she came by, the two of you were snuggling on the couch, talking. As we went by, she smiled, and, in a cooing, yet mocking voice said, 'Ohhh, they are so cute together.' Of course, I felt sort of embarrassed, but I noticed that she kept looking at both of you, the whole time we sat in the kitchen nearby. It was evident to me from her expression that her parents never showed the closeness you two freely expressed and I realized then, how lucky I was, and felt sad for her.

"Ever since I fell in love with Finn, I prayed we'd be able to hold on to that beginning desire and longing that we had when we were first in love; that you and Dad *still* have. But, I see now, how the intense feelings fade. When children and work fill so much of your time, you begin to lose yourself; you struggle to feel desire through all the fatigue. Maybe if I'd spread my little men out, instead of having them so quickly... and then there's work and Zeff's medical issues. Do you think Finn and I can ever get that kind of passion back again?"

Genevieve looked over at Zeff, basking on a raft in the water. Soon after he was born, Ella and Finn noticed differences from the other two boys. Zeff couldn't lift his head easily, even at six months. He wasn't able to sit by himself until he was almost one, and his first few steps didn't come until he was twenty-three months old. By the time he was in kindergarten he was evaluated as delayed, or mildly challenged, mentally. He also had asthma which was controlled pretty well unless he felt overly stressed. Ella took great pains to keep a calm household, even if it meant heightened anxiety for everyone else…as long as Zeff felt no pressure.

In comparing Ella's life to her own, Genevieve only saw apples and oranges. Of course there were pros *and* cons for having children close together or far apart. However, the plethora of situations in life that seem like conflict and struggle, are all a matter of perception. It's a choice to see your life as a victim or victor, whether it is physical or mental.

Genevieve wanted to be thoughtful in answering her daughter, yet, she knew her passion for Teddy had never been compromised by life's conflicts. Maybe it *was* a love for the ages, or an innate attraction for each other, in which angels guided what was meant-to-be. All Genevieve knew for sure was, if love and passion were to endure, it had to be wanted by both. The common desire to hold the other tight and help lift each other up when things got hard; to wipe the tears with a gentle hand, and bask in the happy times, relishing the joy and laughter like a slow-motion movie you hope will never end.

But Ella only needed reassurance, not a sermon. So, Genevieve inquired, "What do you see when you look at Finn?"

Ella looked down and closed her eyes. "I still see the handsome man I married."

Genevieve continued her gentle interrogation, "Now, how do you feel?"

With her eyes still closed, she sat silent for a few moments. Genevieve could see Ella's eyes moving from side to side behind her lids. Then a smile emerged. "I feel special when he smiles at me for no reason at all, or I catch him looking at me from across a crowded room, then pretend like he wasn't. I feel happy watching him rough-house with the boys. I feel comforted when we go together as a couple to see Zeff's doctor. I feel desire for him when I see him sweaty and dirty on the baseball field."

Genevieve laughed, "Okay, Okay. Just remember all of that tonight, after the boys are in bed. Your passion is just fine, my girl. You just needed a little reminder, that's all."

Ella turned a bit flushed and grinned, "I hope I can wait that long."

CHAPTER 46

---- ❦ ----

REMEMBERING THE PAST

GENEVIEVE WATCHED THE baggage handlers loading luggage onto the plane as she sat, looking out her window seat. *I hope I packed enough for both trips.* Figuring two full suitcases would be enough, she turned to watch the people moving down the aisle, trying to find their seats.

As she observed a pregnant woman settling down across the aisle with her young daughter in tow, it reminded Genevieve of the fact she would be a grandmother again soon, as Broc's wife, Adira was seven months pregnant with Genevieve's first granddaughter. A smile crossed Genevieve's face. *Frilly dresses. I need to get a few more on my trip!* Genevieve already had bought several as well as a beautiful, soft pink blanket, and a basketful of baby products and toys. *I just wish they lived a little closer,* Genevieve bemoaned. *But, at least he's happy, and since they only live a few hours away, there's no flying involved!*

As the plane took off and began to soar, Genevieve watched the earth shrink below her. Reminiscing about her first plane ride, long ago, with Uncle Steven and Aunt Melinda, Genevieve closed her eyes. She could still remember the wonder and excitement at seeing everything become so small and seemingly insignificant below; like a toy model world of twinkling lights, intricately designed buildings and miniature cars and trucks that scurried around a make-believe metropolis.

Genevieve's aunt and uncle had been true angels in every way. It made her shudder to think what might have happened to her and Tess if their aunt and uncle weren't there when the world was unraveling around them. But they were, opening up an *incredible* world for the two girls. *I love you two, wherever you are in that vast heaven,* Genevieve lamented, feeling sadness calling, once again. Wiping an escaping tear from her eye, she took a deep breath and grabbed a book to focus on until the plane touched down in Phoenix.

Walking out of the airport with luggage in tow, Genevieve was immediately confronted with a blast of hot Arizona air upon her face. *Yep, feels like home*, she thought with a smirk.

Tess had both arms above her head, waving to get Genevieve's attention. Ryan hurried over, gave Genevieve a kiss, and took the luggage from her hands. "Good timing Gen, we arrived an hour ago and just picked up the rental car."

Genevieve smiled, "Great timing, actually! Thanks for being patient with me, Ryan!"

Ryan, just smiled, "I don't know what you're talking about?"

Arriving at the car, Tess wrapped her arms around Genevieve. "Oh Gen, I know how hard it's been for you, letting go of everything...their legacy, as well as our home, the only real home I ever knew."

As Genevieve held her sister in a tight embrace, she could feel her sister's loss, yet Tess seemed to be moving on with acceptance faster than Genevieve. "I feel *we* are their legacy. I can still remember how it was when we lived with Mom. It wasn't until about a year after moving in with our aunt and uncle that I understood how much we had been blessed. I guess it has been harder than I expected. You never are prepared for such a sudden ending. I think about it every day. Did they suffer in the car accident? It was almost a day before anyone found them down that mountain side.

"Maybe it's the guilt of knowing they had decided to drive to see the family and me. I sensed Uncle Steven wasn't up for the trip, but he is.., was, so stubborn, wanting to visit the central coast, Hearst Castle and then go inland and visit Yosemite for a day or two beforehand. But then, you know all that. I'm glad they were together though. I would hope *that* is how it ends for me someday, next to Teddy." Looking at Tess to assure her she added, "Many years from now of course." Tess frowned. "It better be. Let's talk about something else. This is getting too morbid."

It was catch-up time during the two-hour drive. Genevieve and her sister did their best to get together at least once a year, calling it "sisters' week." And, it was during that time they caught up on a year's worth of living. Since Tess, Ryan, and the girls lived in Florida, full family reunions happened rarely.

Before Genevieve realized it, they were pulling into the beautiful estate. Although Genevieve had been there briefly, during the reading of the will, she chose to stay at a hotel for the funeral, not able to bear staying at her home without the people that made it that way. As Ryan pulled the car up, Gidda, the long-time housekeeper was waiting on the front steps for them. Running over to the car, she grabbed each with a strong bear hug, then everyone helped to move the luggage into the home.

Genevieve had made many visits to her Aunt and Uncle's since she began her life with Teddy, but, as she stepped inside the homey living room where they had all spent so much time as a family, it felt vacant, empty, knowing they weren't there.

But to someone unattached, the room was a warm and inviting gathering place, with a large fireplace and two large picture windows along the north wall which brought in plenty of natural light. A beautiful light blue couch sat in the middle of the room, with a coffee table full of Aunt Melinda's favorite fashion magazines as well as those related to science and astronomy which were Uncle Steven's. A baby grand piano sat silently between the two windows and bookshelves filled tight with novels, covered another wall.

Pictures of Genevieve and Tess at various times of their lives could be found on many of the shelves as well as the family portrait that hung above the mantel, painted of the four of them when Genevieve was thirteen and Tess was five. As Genevieve walked around the room, she spotted a candid picture on a bookshelf of herself with Aunt Melinda and Uncle Steven at Tess's wedding. Genevieve had never seen the picture before. All three were laughing hysterically, and as she picked it up, Genevieve remembered why.

She was sitting with her aunt and uncle in the waiting room of the wedding chapel. Everyone was listening for the cue so that the parents could be seated and the service could begin. Suddenly, the little flower girl was missing. Knowing the music would be starting at any moment, several bridesmaids went scouting around for the little three-year-old. Just as Tess was about to panic, little Kate popped her head out from the back of Tess' gown. Tess never even felt Kate hiding underneath. It got everyone in the room laughing, even Tess, although hers was probably out of relief. Genevieve never realized a photographer was there and snapped that shot. She felt her lip trembling as Tess walked up behind her. "Love that picture! He took one of me too, but fright doesn't look very good on me. I'm glad they didn't frame that one!"

Genevieve turned and smiled. "I still can't believe you couldn't feel the little trickster under your dress!"

Gidda announced she'd have dinner ready in about two hours, so Tess and Ryan went upstairs to freshen up, in Tess' old room, but before Genevieve headed to hers to do the same, she felt the urge to go to the stable.

CHAPTER 47

STABLE SECRETS

WALKING PAST THE large pool, Genevieve thought doing some laps after dinner might do her some good. But, after dipping her feet in lukewarm water, she thought otherwise and headed out, past the manicured lawns finally coming to the stable.

At its peak, it would have been brimming with every breed. Genevieve remembered when all ten stalls were filled. But, now, only one colt remained. A little filly they named Piper. The days of show horses and racing were long gone. When they sold their last stallion a few years back, Uncle Steven mentioned how much he missed that part of his life. Genevieve figured Piper was a way to help fill that void.

Piper looked so lonely, just as Genevieve felt at that moment. She had pondered the possibility of holding on to the estate, maybe even making it an upscale bed and breakfast, and adding a nine-hole golf course to the vast grounds. But as she looked for a sign or feeling of affirmation all she saw was a shadow of what was, and a feeling of loss. Genevieve wandered up and down the dirt aisle as Piper snorted each time she passed.

Genevieve stopped in front of the stall that had been Haddie's, her beloved horse. The stall, like all the others, was dark. A saddle hung just outside, but it wasn't the one Genevieve used with Haddie. As Genevieve looked around the area, that particular saddle wasn't anywhere to be seen, probably long gone now, as was Haddie. Genevieve opened the gate and walked inside. Closing her eyes, Genevieve imagined Haddie was right there, nudging her like she used to do when her horse wanted to ride. Letting out a long sigh, Genevieve thought in resignation, *You can't go back Haddie, can you?*

Just as she started to leave the stall, she heard a hollow noise below her foot. Genevieve looked down. With a puzzled look, she tapped at the ground. *What in the world?* Genevieve got down on her knees and brushed the spot with her hands. When she was done, she stood up and stared down at a small two-foot by two-foot piece of metal. Small hinges on one side, a padlock on the other. *Where did this come from? I used to spend hours in here with Haddie, cleaned the stall by myself all the time, and I know, this wasn't here! What is down there and why is it hidden away like this?* It was getting late, and Genevieve knew she needed to get back to the house. Shuffling hay back over the metal plate, she closed the stall door, kissed Piper on her nose saying, "I'll be back in a little while girl and I'll bring you a couple of carrots." Then Genevieve moved at a fast pace back to the house.

Once there, she ran up the stairs and got ready for dinner. When she came back down, Tess and Ryan were sitting by the pool while Gidda was finishing a salad to go along with the dinner. Noticing that Genevieve seemed anxious, Tess remarked, "Gidda said dinner is almost ready. Are you doing okay?"

Genevieve tried to stay focused. "Oh yes. I just didn't realize how hungry I was, or how tired. I know tomorrow is going to be a long day, so after dinner, I think I'll call it a night if that's okay. Teddy said he'd be calling between 2:00 p.m. and 3:00 p.m. tomorrow to see how everything is going and I hope I can tell him we've made a good dent."

Everyone insisted that Gidda sit at the table so they all could have dinner together. Gidda said she wasn't worried about losing her job there, as several of Aunt Melinda, and Uncle Steven's friends were in a bidding war, trying to win her over. *Of course,* Genevieve thought, *they all know what a catch she would be.* Gidda wasn't just extremely competent, but she had that "mothering" quality about her. She was always ready with a hug if needed and advice, but only if asked, never self-imposed. Genevieve was glad to hear Gidda's future was secured, and wished the other nine full-time employees had the same outlook.

When dinner was finished, Gidda insisted on doing all the cleaning. Genevieve thought about telling Tess what she had found, but she wasn't sure what she wanted to do about it yet, so, decided to wait. After her sister and Ryan had gone upstairs, Genevieve hunted around for a flashlight, crowbar, and a few carrots for Piper. Then under the blanket of night, she headed back to the stable.

Surprising Piper with her appearance, the filly took a startled step back and whinnied. Turning on her flashlight, Genevieve whispered, "It's okay girl. Sorry to startle you." Piper stepped up to the gate, and Genevieve offered one of the carrots which Piper happily started to munch on. Stroking the bridge of her nose, Genevieve stared down at Haddie's old stall. When Piper had eaten all the carrots, Genevieve let the flashlight guide her to her destination. Brushing the hay away, she knelt down and stared at the lock. *Hidden secrets, locked away...why? Will it be a hidden treasure or something that I'll regret the rest of my life?* Genevieve felt her heart throbbing. *I could just walk away, let things be.* But Genevieve reasoned if she weren't supposed to see what was inside, she never would have found it. So, she took the crowbar and without much effort pried the lock off.

Holding the flashlight in one hand, she lifted the metal plate. Inside was a metal tool box wrapped in plastic. Genevieve reached down to pull it out. As she grabbed the handle, bracing for a heavy lift, she almost fell backward, it felt empty inside. Unwrapping the plastic, she lifted the latch. On top was a thick notebook, below, various papers and pictures. Genevieve moved to the side of the stall with the box and sat leaning up against the boards. Taking the notebook out, she opened to the first page. It was Uncle Steven's writing. *He must have had a secret from Aunt Melinda if he had to hide it out here. But what? He was always an open book, and they were so happy together, to the end. Why was he compelled to hide something from her?* Genevieve reasoned she had a duty to her aunt to know the truth and began to read.

CHAPTER 48

IN HIS OWN WORDS

NOT ONE THAT feels compelled to write my feelings, yet I have no one I can talk to, so, as a way to self-console as well as have a record, should it ever be needed in the future, this will have to do.

Melinda and I are to be married next month. She is my everything, a blessing from the moment I met her.

Last night, she was raped.

As I write the words, I feel so sick. She knows who it is, but she won't tell me, afraid I would kill him, and she's right, I wouldn't hesitate. She won't go to the police, feeling so ashamed. I don't know what to do. But, somehow, I'm going to find out who it is and kill him!

Genevieve couldn't believe what she was reading. Turning, she became ill, and tears filled her eyes. *This can't be true. Did my mother ever know what happened?* The only way she might get more answers would be to read on.

Next entry:

Melinda is hurting and I don't know what to do for her. She said she understands if I want to call off the marriage, but that is farthest from my mind. She refuses to tell me who did this to her as she can see the rage I have and said, in the end, it would be her word against his. Her stomach is upset all the time and somehow, she feels guilty, saying if she didn't have the job she had, maybe it wouldn't have happened. I've tried to narrow down who it might be, but, as a model, she has so many contacts and her pictures are everywhere. I've decided to back off for now. I wish I knew what to do.

A model. She always looked like one to me, but never once said anything about having been one. As Genevieve looked at some of the pictures, at the bottom, she found several of her aunt. She was gorgeous. There were a few headshots, pictures on runways and glamor shots with dramatic make-up. But one took Genevieve's breath away. It was one of her and Uncle Steven. It was a candid shot when she must have been on a modeling shoot. It was a close-up of the two in a passionate kiss. Genevieve smiled, *Such a romantic picture. This should be framed in their living room, not hidden away in obscurity.* Turning the page, she continued to read the next entry.

We are to be married in two days and Melinda told me she's pregnant. She said she didn't deserve me and tried to call off the wedding, saying I'd never be able to see her like I used to. I thought she knew me better than that. I of course refused. I asked her if she was going to keep the baby and she just cried. I don't know what that means or if she even knows what to do yet. Either way, I'll be here for her, no matter what.

I can't imagine what they went through. Pregnant. I was always told Aunt Melinda couldn't have children. Did she do something desperate to cause that? Why didn't they ever tell me about this?

Turning the page,

In spite of the circumstance, the wedding was incredible. Melinda took my breath away, she's so beautiful. Even though she's dealing with morning sickness, I think she really enjoyed the day.

Part of the reason is that she's made up her mind about the baby. She said that although it will be hard, she wants to carry the baby to term. However, she said she couldn't keep it. The baby deserved a mother who only looked to the future. Melinda believes that she would end up resenting the child, as would I, always looking at the past. I don't know if I would or not, but it's her child, her decision.

Genevieve had seen their wedding pictures before, but Uncle Steven had placed one in the box as well. It was one where they both had huge smiles and were toasting something; champagne glasses raised high. *Were they toasting the bride and groom's future? Did you smile imagining you'd have children of your own?*

Genevieve turned the page:

I found out who the father was today. His name is Godfrey Jigstone, a photographer. I only know because now that Melinda is five months pregnant she thought enough time had passed and I had gotten beyond the fury I had felt. But, hard as I try, it is always there, simmering. She told me because he had found out she was pregnant and approached her when she was shopping, to verify he was the father. When he found out he was, he asked if she planned to keep the baby. When Melinda said no, that she had contacted an adoption agency, he pleaded with her to give the baby to him. She refused, saying he had no right to be blessed with something so precious after what he did.

It took a few calls to find out where this miscreant lived. Although his home is in England, he has an apartment here, so I went yesterday to pay him a visit. It was all I could do not to kill him, but, let's just say, his nose now tilts to the side. I told him I'd be watching him from now on, and if he approached

Melinda ever again, I wouldn't hesitate to kill him. Before I left, he said he regretted terribly what he had done. Never had he done anything like that before and loathed himself for hurting her like that. He said when he found out he might be the father, all he could think about was the baby. He wants to be a father to the child now that Melinda is giving it away. I told him just because you can father a child, doesn't make you father material. I told him, 'if you can rape someone, what holds you back from other impulses?' I said I would never trust that he would have the child's best interest in mind or be able to truly love it like it deserved. Then I left.

I can't tell Melinda about this. She would be furious if she knew I confronted him, but I wonder if she would have any solace in knowing he was remorseful. Maybe he told her, I don't know.

Genevieve could see Teddy doing the same thing. The two were more alike than she had realized. She had never seen an angry side to her uncle. Sure, he used a few choice words when a bid fell through, which was rare, and she and Tess learned just how far to stretch the boundaries before Uncle Steven would lay down the law and ground them for their bad behavior. But in all their time together, Genevieve couldn't recall a time that Uncle Steven showed any anger toward her aunt. In fact, she couldn't even remember a single argument between the two.

Moving to the next page,

The baby was born today. It's a girl. At first, I didn't want to see her, but, after all, she's part Melinda. She's got a lot of dark hair and looks healthy. We met with the couple who will be adopting her last week. Melinda and I have a good feeling about them. They will take the baby home tomorrow. Then Melinda and I can move past this for good. I can tell she feels

191

sad. She didn't want to see the baby when it was born, which was probably a good thing. She just knows it's a healthy girl and she seems satisfied with that.

Next page:

I was getting ready to pick up Melinda from the hospital and the phone rang. It was the case worker at the adoption agency. I could tell she was really upset. She said a man claiming to be the father was contesting the adoption, and petitioning sole custody of the infant.

We had confided in the case worker that Melinda had been raped. What she didn't know was that Melinda knew who the rapist was and that he had wanted the baby for himself. I had hoped that my visit had put some sense into him, at least I had hoped. The case worker said when she talked to the gentleman, named Godfrey, she confronted him with the allegation which he denied, saying it was true that he and Melinda had made a mistake, however, it was consensual. He said he would gladly take a paternity test if it were needed.

All I knew was that I wanted to spare Melinda from any further heartache. She had released her hold on any rights to the baby and now it looked like, fitting or not, Godfrey would end up taking the baby. I told the case worker how sorry I was, that Melinda and I had been comforted in knowing the baby was going to a good home. But I also told her if Melinda found out that the person that raped her, was now getting custody of that baby, it would kill her. The case worker agreed, saying she'd never talk to Melinda again, and said she'd speak to the distraught couple as well, but, she said, the biological father might not be so caring of her feelings. After all, none of this would have happened if he did.

She was right about that. That's why I'm going to see him now.

CHAPTER 49

―――― ⌘ ――――

BLESS THE MAN

GENEVIEVE HAD TO stop reading and let everything sink in. *How very sad and lonely it must have been for Uncle Steven to shoulder such a burden and have no one to talk to about it.* Reading his personal thoughts was like getting to know him all over again, but on a much deeper level. *Did he ever expect anyone to discover all this? Of all the places he could have hidden it, why did he decide to put it here, in Haddie's stall.* Questions swirled in her mind. But, as she got ready to read the next entry, she knew there were more revelations to come.

As soon as Godfrey opened the door, he jumped back. But punching him in the face again wasn't going to solve anything now. I told him I would allow him to move forward unobstructed with two stipulations.

1. He moves far away and never lets Melinda know he has their daughter.
2. I want constant proof that he is taking good care of the girl, with pictures, school grades, activities, hobbies and anything else to show me I'm wrong about him.

I gave him a P.O Box and said I *only*, want to know where they have moved to, and if he doesn't comply, he knows I have the resources to hunt him down, and that would be a big mistake on his part.

I'm going to pick up my wife now. Maybe I'll take her to her favorite restaurant "Mario's" for a drink and some good lasagna.

So, she never knew. That's why Uncle Steven hid everything away, still needing to know his wife's little girl was going to be safe and loved. God, I wish I could give you a hug right now, Uncle! Genevieve ran her fingers along her uncle's words, wishing she could feel what he felt so long ago.

There were only a few more entries. Next page,

The more I thought about it, I wanted more proof than just photos, so I hired Tom Bardon, a private investigator that came highly recommended by a colleague of mine. The baby is six months old now, and although I have received two pictures, I wanted to see how he was treating her. The investigator contacted me last week with his report and sent photos of Godfrey with the baby that I received today. Tom said the father dotes on the child, takes her on walks and treats her like she's a china doll. He has bought everything a baby could ever want and has a nanny stay with her when he works. I won't keep these pictures because, and although, I'm satisfied with the investigation, I still can't stomach to look at the guy.

I understand you taking the extra step. Pictures are just a still moment in time, and can never tell the whole story. How could you really trust the man when the only thing you knew about his character was despicable? You did all you could, an invisible angel the little one would never know.

Next page,

Godfrey sent me a newspaper clipping today. It was a wedding announcement and picture of himself and his new bride. I suppose he sent it to me to let me know the little girl would have a mother now. She's almost three years old. The last picture I received was of her and Mickey Mouse a few weeks ago. She looks happy. I tossed the clipping, but I'm glad he let me know.

Genevieve started to go through the pictures and papers in the box. *The cousin I never knew.* Picking up the last picture in the box and the first one ever sent, Genevieve gazed at a baby, maybe two months old with curly dark hair, and a cute smile. On the back it said, **Faye 2 ½ months old.** *Faye was Aunt Melinda's middle name. How did you feel about that, Uncle Steven?*

Going from one picture to another, Faye looked happy and healthy. By the time she was five years old, Genevieve could see that Faye was looking more and more like her mother, Melinda. She received mostly good grades in school, except for history and biology which seemed to be a constant struggle for her. *We sure had that in common,* Genevieve mused. There were pictures of Faye at the piano, swimming in a pool, at a school prom, and running track. By all accounts, it looked like Godfrey had proven Uncle Steven wrong, which had to be comforting in an odd way.

The pictures ended with a wedding picture of Faye and her groom. On the back it said, **Now Faye and Dillon Greer.**

There was only one other thing in the box. A newspaper clipping. It was quite faded. It was an obituary of Faye Greer. She was forty-one, a single car accident on a mountain road that happened at night. *The same fate as her mother.* Genevieve never knew her cousin but couldn't help feeling a loss, not to mention all the times her aunt probably looked at Genevieve or Tess and wondered about her own daughter.

There was only one other entry in the notebook:

It's been a long time, but it looks like Melinda is ready to be a mother again. I'm really excited to see how I will fare at fatherhood. We found out today that Melinda's brother-in-law has just died. I had only met him a couple of times, but he seemed like a really good guy, a real patriot. Anyway, so we're headed there for a few days, to attend the funeral. But when we get back, it's baby making time!

As tears rolled down Genevieve's face, she whispered, *"I hope I made you proud. You made one hell of a fantastic dad."*

Genevieve realized now that it was no accident that she just happened to stumble onto something so important to her uncle--she *was* meant to find it. There were plenty of places in the house that Aunt Melinda had no interest in going, ever; places to hide that part of their life until they were both gone. But he didn't want everyone to know, just Genevieve, hoping she would discover it one day, in the place he knew she always went when she felt lost and searched for answers.

Along with the notebook, Genevieve gathered the pictures of her aunt modeling, and the one with her aunt and uncle kissing, but only one of Faye. It was the one taken at her school prom, and she was the mirror image of her mother. Setting them aside, she walked behind the stable where several old barrels sat. Throwing all the rest of the pictures and documents inside one of them, she went to the tool shed and found some matches. Returning to the barrel, she burned what was past.

The courage my aunt had, to carry a child conceived through rape, and then the continued love and concern my uncle had for his wife's child is the best legacy they could have ever given me. Thank you, thank you for telling me, Uncle.

Back at the house, Genevieve walked into the living room and turned on the lights. Grabbing two of the many pictures of her, displayed around the room, she began to replace them. First with her aunt and uncle in their loving embrace, the other with her aunt, dramatic and elegant, walking the runway in a sparkling red gown.

When Genevieve was finished, she gathered up the notebook and remaining pictures and walked to the door. Turning, she paused to look at her aunt and uncle, a kiss, frozen in time. With a satisfied smile, she turned off the lights and headed to bed.

PART SEVEN

MOVING ON

CHAPTER 50

TRUE REALITY

THE CHOICES SHE reflected upon were now over.

Still lying on the couch, she opened her eyes and the elaborate illusion of Genevieve's life was starting to fade. Besides the ornate clock on the wall and the fire in the fireplace, continuing to give off a comforting glow, the room had begun to dissolve in transparency. As she looked around, all those that had attended her party were surrounding her, still reflecting the human personality each had portrayed, but now, slowing reverting into their natural luminescence.

Her angel, sitting by her side, still masquerading as Rosa, held her hand. The pretense of having to speak in words was unnecessary now, as thoughts were immediately understood among them all. *We all had such fun spending your **birth day** this way, my cherished Sapphira. It was a wonderfully whimsical and unique way to prepare for your upcoming physical life as Genevieve.*

The Life-Force or Soul, known as Sapphira, looked around at all the fellow Souls she had grown close to over many, many lifetimes. She could feel the satisfaction they had, playing a part in her preparation fantasy; even going so far as to replace the name they had known her as, in *their* lifetime together, and replacing it with Genevieve to instill a realism to her illusion.

Amanda, her childhood friend from Sapphira's previous life, (in which Sapphira had lived as Justine), sensed Sapphira's extreme pleasure that everyone played along so flawlessly, and commented, *As each of us arrived at the party, Rosa was there to greet us. She impressed the importance that, from that moment on, you were only Genevieve, to us. You don't know how many times, during my story, I almost called you Justine!*

Then Jay, interjected, *At least she was a female in your lifetime together. It was quite a challenge to remember to say Genevieve, when she was my buddy, my hero, Tobias in our lifetime together!* Sapphira's facial expression showed more than words ever could, as she cast her extreme thankfulness to everyone for playing along and staying in character.

Suddenly, a flash of brilliance illuminated the room. When Sapphira turned her head, the illusion of Rosa had disappeared, and her Guardian Angel Ziia was looking tenderly down at her. Ziia's radiating aura would be inconceivable to the human eye. Angels tasked with the intricate care of the Souls they guard, are given extraordinary luminosity by Source, or, otherwise known to humans as God, Jehovah, Krishna, El Shaddai, Allah and a host of others. No matter the name given Source, the omniscient, and undefinable I AM THAT I AM, blesses the angels with exquisite radiance and powers of perception that are incomprehensible, even to the Souls in their care.

Always in awe of the blessing that was Ziia, Sapphira couldn't imagine doing all that she did without her. Over eons, Ziia helped Sapphira in countless adventures; preparing her, guiding her, and *always* bringing comfort in many disguised ways, when the path forward, in time and space, seemed obscured.

The Soul, or Life-Force, knows that time is irrelevant when true reality is eternal. Each venture into the physical is but a brief moment. Sapphira likened each lifetime to a day trip. A short, but much-anticipated excursion to experience someone and some place as never before.

Sapphira had made many of those trips, on Earth alone. Once, life as an ancient man; another as a tortured rebel in the Ming Dynasty. The Soul's life as a Celtic warrior loved freely (both men and women), while the life as a cloistered nun dwelt only in the spiritual love of the highest power. The Life-Force now understood, first-hand, the dangers lived as a beggar with no family and no home; as well as dangers of a different sort, that came from extreme wealth and status. Sapphira expanded greatly when living a disabled life without hearing, and another with debilitating schizophrenia. There were lives that only lasted a few days or years, and others that carried the Soul well past one-hundred. And, for each and every life, the Soul grew wiser with experience, maturity more evident in the lives it inhabited.

But, of all the adventures lived thus far, it was the life experienced as a Roman slave that still resonated the most with the Soul. The slave's name was Sapphira, the fourteen-year-old daughter of a poor widowed iron worker. In that time, extortion, as well as high taxes collected by the local publican, were crushing everyone in the area. Soon, Sapphira and her father would lose the small dirt dwelling they called home. Watching her father agonize over their situation, and exhausted from endless work, Sapphira knew there was a choice she had to make, hard as it would be.

An arrogant Senate aristocrat by the name of Marcius Caldus had taken notice of Sapphira several times while in the local marketplace. He was unabashed in his advances toward her. To keep her father from losing the little he had left, Sapphira kept a watch for the Senator. Upon seeing him one day as he was buying a bracelet for his wife, Sapphira approached him with a proposition. She would agree to any position of which he would take her if he would pay off the tax burden of her father. Marcius agreed without hesitation. Sapphira, even at her young age had no illusion of what Marcius had planned for her.

Before she left her father, never to see him again, he sat holding Sapphira tight in his arms and wept. Kissing him gently on his forehead, she reminded him that he had raised her to be strong and to trust that she would always be alright. That very night Marcius sent a servant to deliver the money, adding even more than was agreed upon, and then collected his newest acquisition.

Sapphira, endowed with an innocent beauty, became Marcius' favored concubine. With her soothing, gentle nature, the slaves within the house soon looked to her for counsel and comfort. Just before she reached eighteen, Sapphira met and quickly fell in love with a male slave that had just been bought by Marcius. His name was Ionas. For more than a decade they lived and loved in secret.

One day, just before Sapphira's twenty-ninth birthday she was told that her owner, Marcius, had found out about her relationship with Ionas and was in an uncontrolled rage. Urged to try and flee, Sapphira knew there was nowhere she could hide. So, she found Ionas, and they spent the last remaining hours passionately loving each other; always knowing that one day they would pay for the love they were helpless to deny.

When Marcius found them, he took great satisfaction in killing Ionas first, while Sapphira watched helplessly. As Marcius was just about to plunge a knife deep into Sapphira's chest, a strange calm came over her. Instead of looking at the distorted furor on her owner's face, she instead fixated upon Ionas' lifeless body as it lay next to hers. She could still feel his love and knew he was quite alright, and that she would be as well.

Although the Soul has no gender, most choose to reflect a personality previously lived that epitomizes all that love can be. That was how it was for the Soul called Sapphira.

It was also that same life as a slave, in which Sapphira experienced as never before, or after, such an intense, transcending love as was felt for Ionas. Now, once again Sapphira would be drawn to that same Life-Force, already on his earthly adventure as Theodore (Teddy) Walker. It was something that had been planned enthusiastically by both Souls.

CHAPTER 51

———— ∞᠎᠎᠎᠎᠎᠎᠎᠎᠎᠎᠎᠎ ————

BEGINNING OF A DAY TRIP

KNOWING THAT BABY Genevieve was about to be born, Ziia impressed upon Sapphira, *Each life, as you know, is fluid…every moment ever changing. Yet, there are always those high probabilities in which I may be helpful. There are five major choices I could foresee for Genevieve that are likely to be encountered. Of each, there is a road that will ultimately be the easier one, taking you along the path you have chosen to experience. The other, as you've taken many times before, a rather bumpy one.* Sapphira looked at Ziia with a guilty grin and sensed quite a bit of amusement coming from those around her as well.

As you rested, I empowered you with the knowledge that would result from each choice. You are well aware of them now. But, as you take your first breath as Genevieve, all that understanding will be forgotten. When each event unfolds, and a choice is to be made, the very cells of your body will whisper to you in their own way, for they will hold this knowledge. Guidance will come as you experience a powerful urge or what humans call Deja vu.

But, no matter the choice you ultimately make, you are never alone my brave Sapphira. I will always be as near as the air around you, anticipating your every move. A host of angels, as well as all those that surround you here and many on Earth now, will be at your beck and call, just as it is for every precious Soul that leaves this comfort for difficult and sometimes unimaginable trials that are endured in time and space.

As you know though, it is in those trials; the contrast we never experience here, that Source loves you beyond measure. For what you experience, Source experiences, when you triumph, Source triumphs. And when you feel beat down from the conflicts that surround you, Source trusts in us to help lift you up. We all are in this together, my Love. Sapphira needed Ziia's comforting thoughts now as everything was fading from view. She couldn't feel the touch of Ziia's hand anymore. Ziia slowly bent down to kiss Sapphira. *Good-bye for now, my dear friend.*

For Sapphira, the Soul's integration with Genevieve was coming to completion. The pain of physical birth was evident, as the excruciating pressure of the physical body being born was also intensely felt by the Soul. For, not only was Sapphira experiencing the body's senses profoundly now, but she also was in the final stages of relinquishing the boundless, non-physical freedom, for the difficult restrictions of being bound to a physical body. It would take months for the Life-Force to completely acclimate to a physical existence.

The love directed upon Sapphira by all those surrounding her felt like a drug, helping her through the difficult process. Then, as the final push was about to sever the connection with the loved ones around her, Sapphira felt ecstasy. The Eternal Source was penetrating her Soul with an unspeakable, ineffable love; blessing the journey as Genevieve.

Sapphira was gone.

One by one the Souls acknowledged their love to Ziia and disappeared in a flash of light. Soon, Ziia sat alone on the couch. After a few moments, she stood up and looked at the clock. Silence was all around. She watched for several seconds, then...tick, tock. The hand moved, and Genevieve's life had begun.

Ziia, moved around the room and took a last look before it too disappeared. Stopping to look at the first photo, she recalled Sapphira's short life as a Peruvian boy. While learning to catch fish by hand in a shallow stream, he was bitten by a Fer-de-Lance snake, leaving Earth at the young age of six. Each of Sapphira's life journeys hung on the wall like cherished awards.

But one of Ziia's favorite pictures was of the life Sapphira lived as Ayana, on a small Caribbean island. An uneventful life, compared to most, but a serene one all the same. Ayana lived a blissful existence as a wife and mother when island life reveled in pure, unadulterated simplicity. It was also Sapphira's longest life, returning home at one-hundred and twelve. The picture was of

Ayana at about twenty-five, eternally frozen in time with a loving gaze upon her newborn son. She was sitting in a rocking chair on the front porch of her small, two-room beach cottage. In the foreground, the picture captured the sun's hazy red glow as it was peeking up on the horizon, casting a glittery shimmer on the azure ocean water.

As Ziia touched the picture, she released its energy and watched it disappear, back into the endlessness of the universe. She marveled at the perfection Source had devised for all to create their reality as well as all the things within it. Whether angel or flesh and bone, by divine law, once the invisible energy is summoned by a consciousness, it *will* create flawlessly upon the thoughts that attracted it. Ziia couldn't help but grin, imagining all the mischief Genevieve might attract with her brazen Soul, Sapphira cheering her on. *Be careful what you think and dwell on, my darling Genevieve!*

By the time Ziia arrived at the fireplace, nothing but it remained of Sapphira's illusion. Ziia had taken great enjoyment in planning the fantasy birthday with Sapphira, as well as devising her own unique character as a human caregiver. She also knew that, before long, the two would be conspiring once again to prepare for yet another life. But for now, the faint cries were getting louder, and Ziia's attention belonged with baby Genevieve.

Looking down at the mellowing fire, Ziia gave a sly smile. *One more light to blow out,* she pondered in amusement. Then, pretending to take in a deep breath Ziia gave a swift puff, and everything went dark.

For more insights on this book as well as information on the upcoming sequel,
Please visit: www.SherylMFrazer.com

Proof

Made in the USA
Columbia, SC
18 December 2017